DIGITAL SPHERE

& Phobia

WITH THE MYTHOLOGY OF THE DANCE OF THE LION

All Those Who Must Go Far In Life Must Welcome And Embrace The Technology for Flight And for Freedom. No One Can Truly Fly Without Technology

Technology, Adventures, History, Exposures, Mythology, Satire, Science…

Chinenyike Ezemagu

1

TABLE OF CONTENTS

Author's Note

The story is about a powerful and progressive household called Edoga. It is centered or focused on a boy child called Obi and his inappropriate indulgence in phone gadget and the general fears, anxiety and strong reservation that accompany the use of modern technology, technological device and internet space which is perceived and judged as the chief harbinger and cause of the destruction of youths and the younger generation.

Obi's abuse of phone technology and the perceived criminality culminated and led to a long family assembly and deliberations to resolve and find a healthy solution to the crisis, fear and grief that have visited the noble home unannounced. Nobody anticipated the strange event in the life of the lad. But all anticipation is uniform among all the members of the family: to reach a happy resolution.

Digital Sphere is essentially about technological revolution. It is a critique and exposition of culture lag and extreme culture lag in technological knowledge and digital development. It aims to make a salient point which is that, notwithstanding the existential and enormous fears and crises associated with technological device, phone technology and internet space especially in the life of the younger generations, the way forward cannot be withdrawal, isolation, denial, rejection and flight from modern technology, exposure, progressive advancement, meaningful adventures and critical innovations. For those who fear the bees cannot have the honey.

CHINENYIKE EZEMAGU

THE 'GREEK ASSEMBLY'

1

Within our own time and space when the power of science has not only circumvented and defied the law of gravity to be able to suspend big and strong metal in the air for hours; but ultimately a time when technological gadgets and microchips are the new toys with which children played with and internet space is the new 'Greek assembly' which virtually everyone attended and participated in, there lived a powerful household called Edoga. There lived a progressive and Godly family in the biggest country of the second largest continent in the world.

Within the family, in the morning, there was a 'Greek assembly' that featured every member of the family inclusively. But the family Greek assembly today's morning was not hosted on the internet, yet it was everything about and revolved around the internet space and phone gadgets and how they have affected and damaged the young ones.

Even at that, the debate appeared stronger and more successful on the strength, advantage, usefulness, validity and acceptance of technological revolution with its attendant gadgets for the use and benefits of everyone regardless of the phobia and dubiety, regardless of age. It was only Ebube, among all, that appeared so troubled and pained with the recent event in his society.

'Did you not learn how, in recent time, a popular politician mocks his own people and boasts confidently over the backwardness of his people rejoicing that the people do not know about internet space and its use even in this technological era?' Ebube asked Mrs Veronica looking at her in the face.

'I did not believe this statement is true until you brought it up now again'

'But whether or not the statement was made by the politician, it is of lesser consequence. What is more important is the truth that our people have long lagged behind technologically and digitally; our people have suffered too bad and we have a duty to do something about it fast to raise their status, liberate them and salvage this new low'

'Very true. Yet, it is still revealing that our leaders celebrate the backwardness of the people, willfully keeping this nation underdeveloped and retarded'

'They fear how the technology can transform them and make them even superior than them so they intentionally keep the people poor for their own victory, for their own benefits and interests'

'They know too well that they cannot win if the people are exposed, aware and well equipped. They know what the weapon of technology can do for the people and they fear to grow and install it'

'Instead, they choose to weaponize poverty, backwardness and underdevelopment. They fear the real weapon. The weapon of technology'

'Yes, their weapon for victory and continual sit-tight in power is keeping the people backward, ignorant and wretched; it is not technology, it is not progress'

'They do not know that there is no weapon on the face of the earth as powerful and effective as building technology and digital advancement'

'It is certainly not something any right thinking person or well-meaning politician would think of, let alone to spill it out in the public and boast of the technological backwardness of his people, the 90% of people who are not yet exposed to digital space, internet technology and the general technological revolution infiltrating and penetrating all parts of the world'

'Yes, I do agree with you. Yet, we do not have to cry over spilt milk. If he has mocked the people shamelessly and boasted of their digital backwardness, I think we should take it as a challenge to reinvest in our people, to rebuild and develop them technologically and otherwise through our own little efforts', Ebube begged and submitted.

The popular or traditional voice feared the new device, digital technology or internet space and accused it of destructions - destroying the new generation. Yet, like a twist of skimet, all votes went for technology. The people began gradually, after a deeper conversation, to see differently and to understand that everyone must develop and build technologically.

TECHNOLOGY OF FLIGHT
AND FRIGHT

2

March, 2021

Living Room,

Edoga's Residence

Within the household of Edoga, like it was in the old days of Eden and Job, the devil's presence was felt. The members of the family were greeted by grief and fear in the early morning. But nobody was dead. Even so, a very dear soul was perceived to be lost or dead. Lost to the pit of hell. Lost to the devil and its empty shows and vanities. Phone and internet were perceived and judged to be the empty shows, vanities, pit of hell and even satanic and demonic. But not every member of the house supported this (dangerous) bill or ruling because it was not progressive and innovative. Not in the glorious Age of science and technology. Not in the wake and splendor of scientific revolution and technological transformations. Not surely in the brilliant time of phone gadgets and internet, information and communication, intelligence and learning. No one can turn back the hands of time.

Aware of the danger threatening the family this morning, every member was addressed and highly exhorted in a strong religious mood to draw strength from the words and teaching of the Apostle many centuries ago in the dead past which Africa cannot relate with, neither in time nor space. Alertness and sobriety of mind and putting on the armor of faith became the necessary call for strong and intense resistance against the scorpion-demon which has shown out its stinging tail, and the entire family has come together and stood united to see that it did not get at its targeted victim. It was the unsafe lifestyle of an only son.

Finding out Obi's possession of a powerful and expensive device threatened severely his freedom and chances of keeping gadgets. A sweet and lovely family gathering that came with its regular attendant dramas and amusement suddenly went sour and stale. A clarion call for a longer family assembly and deliberations was decided for the deliverance of the family; for the redemption of Obi.

It was not just mere coincidence when Obi's father read from the two books of Genesis and Job to admonish the entire house that since the old days of the garden of Eden and the gathering of the household of Job, the devil had always wandered in search of who to devour; the devil had not rested or got tired of troubling the sons and daughters of God and causing destructions and pains in the world. He was invariably speaking to a soul. He was speaking to all but his message was more particular to one person. That particular soul was Obi the only son.

Today everyone was seated in good mood for a very happy family conference for prayers in the morning just as usual except for one danger that has suddenly popped up and surfaced taking almost everybody unaware. For no clear reason, Obi was already putting his belonging where his hand could not reach. The carrying of the shoulder high would easily destroy Obi if nothing was done promptly and smartly about it. Was it not taught in all times and Ages that pride goes before a fall? It was gravely feared that Obi might not end well; Obi's fate might not be different from the Greek Icarus. The child was biting more than he could chew.

Obi first learnt about the curious but pathetic story of the Greek Icarus from his Dad two weeks ago when the latter was driving the former to school on Monday morning. The father had readily judged and hoped too much that the popular Greek tale would offer some moral to his erring son and to help him to retrace his steps and turn a new leaf. He kick-started the discussion from the Greek mythology.

'Have you heard of the Greek Icarus'. The father inquired in a low but firm tone thereby interrupting the long silence father and son had observed almost soberly since they drove out of the house.

'No, I don't know about any Icarus or rather Greek Icarus, you said' He was rather nonchalant.

The father stared at Obi with a long face. He missed his driving and almost smashed another car but he swiftly regained control and refocused attention. Like all adolescents and like Icarus in the Greek story, Obi had all his life struggled frantically with parental advice. Obviously, the father was not impressed with his performance at the question. But had he ever been impressed about Obi? By the way, it was all about his questionable character and conduct-likely to ruin his life as well as the entire family and also do serious damage to the society that the father has obliged to engage him in a *tete a tete*; fatherly instruction.

The father had started off with an old age Igbo proverb, *ekwughi ekwu negbu okenyi, ma ogbu ekwughe anughi nebu nwata*. The exordium was filled with aphorisms and maxims. 'Also, our people say many years ago that an adult does not stay at home to see a she-goat give birth. So, you can't possibly ruin when I am still in the house; when I am still alive and the head of this very family'. Obi knew, from all indications, the father was out for his usual counsel. And a very long and serious one at that! The generality of the atmosphere, the long, grand silence and dubious mood all throughout the morning made him to understand better and prepare and condition his mind for some hard talk, long talk. His poor performance with the Icarus question did not do much to douse the already tensed atmosphere. He was fully aware he had fallen his father's hand. He had again disappointed him.

'It is clear that your reading culture is below expectation. You are just about to graduate from the college, yet you know nothing about the popular Greek Icarus. I want you to do more readings. Readers are leaders'

Inwardly, notwithstanding the early morning wise counsel, Obi was distracted in his head with all the slogans he had gathered from the streets, 'who book help, who school help? School na scam! Dad, stop the lie. I know too well where the readers in our country are found. They are never leaders. They are not even employed let alone being leaders'

Resuming the Icarus subject matter, in quick minutes, the father related the terrible fate of the Greek Icarus who flew so high and was so overwhelmed, infatuated, deluded and drifted away flying beyond the height he should not and got destroyed by the heat of the sun which melt its wax. On the island of Crete thousands of years ago, there was a man named Daedalus. Daedalus had a son called Icarus. It was during the reign of king Minos.

The father of Icarus was and lived like every man in the land. Except that he was endowed and blessed with the power of certain inventions of powerful mechanics. The mechanics were to the ancient world what modern technology is today. The gifting of one of his mechanical creations by Daedalus to the newborn princess to celebrate her birth had suddenly became the news everywhere in the land. It brought Daedalus to the limelight and endeared him so much to Minos the king. The gift was a tiny mechanical bird that squeaked at the rising of the sun. It should be recalled that this was a time the life of man on earth was still very crude and very little or no inventions and innovations had penetrated the universe. People walked all distances with no cars except horses or carriage which was a luxury for the rich. No clocks too but sundials. Even in the near modern world, the clever Galileo could only employ ingeniously his own heart palpitation to keep count of his calculation of the movement of the pendulum of the lamp back and forth at the cathedral at Pisa.

It was not surprising therefore that Daedalus stormed his world and shocked it with his innovation as a mountain of a champion. The king approached and asked him for another invention. The task that had befallen Daedalus was to build a giant labyrinth to hold the half-man and half-bull monster called the Minotaur, prisoner. Daedalus accepted it. But he would have perhaps decided better if he had known the intention of the king. The king bore the symbol of monopoly and wanted Daedalus to work only for him. He was fearful to let the idea escape and spread around. He kept Daedalus prisoner without wanting him to impart the knowledge to any others. The king was everything greedy and so he had his royal guards to take Daedalus and his young son, Icarus, and lock them away in a cave high above the sea. The only entrances to the cave were through the labyrinth guarded by the king's soldiers and an entrance overlooking the sea high up on the side of a cliff.

Left only to Daedalus, his imprisonment did not matter much to him. He seemed happy with it living his life and doing that which he knew how to do best – invention and invention. While the king provided him with virtually everything he needed. Food, drinks, tools of all shapes, rare metals, leather, parchment and even candles so he could work late into the night. The only time things changed and Daedalus began to reconsider the lifestyle he had lived for many years was when his son rebelled. The young Icarus was many times bored having only to keep himself happy only with helping out his father and playing with the mechanical toys Daedalus made for him. And Icarus, being tired of the cold, damp cave, had started to complain and protest strongly against staying further in the cave which threatened seriously the hope of him possessing a life of his own.

It was during the sixteenth birthday anniversary of Icarus that the celebrant could no longer hold back his emotions and finally found outlet for them. He yelled before his father,

'But father, I want an adventure. I seek my own adventure – maybe even to meet a girl and prepare for my own family. I can't very well ask a wife to come to live with me in this lonely cave over the sea. I hate this cave. I hate the king. And I hate you'

Icarus' bold protest birthed eventually the freedom of father and son. It was not until the incidence that Daedalus began to wonder if being locked away was the best thing for his son and for him too. His eyes gradually began to open to freedom, to a liberation he had long taken for granted. But Icarus also did find it consequential to apologize to his father later for the strong utterances he had leveled against his father. But also, he maintained his stance on gaining freedom.

When next the king Minos visited the cave, Daedalus transferred his son's anger coupled with his to the king. Daedalus pleaded, 'your majesty, surely you must see that Icarus is becoming a young man. you can't plan to keep him locked away for his entire life. Please sir, let him join your royal guard and seek a life in your service'.

Of course, no tyrant or dictator in history had welcomed and rejoiced at the liberation of his victims, and so was king Minos who blew hot, raised an eyebrow and gave Daedalus a long look with a strange countenance that seemed to be saying, 'you shall burn to death here and regret the moment you started to entertain thoughts and desires that challenge my supreme authority and sovereignty'.

There was no gain insisting that Daedalus did not expect something different from the king. He did not underestimate the weight and cost of what he was asking. He did not have to stay long thinking about it. He knew right away that the king did not want their liberation. He knew that the king could fear that Icarus had gathered so much knowledge and experience from staying with him, watching and learning the arts and this was what the greedy king feared most, he did not want any others to share in the knowledge Daedalus had. Under no circumstances, did the king want another kingdom to get their hands on the mechanical wonders Daedalus created which Icarus might one day recreate. When the king came visiting again, he told Daedalus, 'Icarus provides the greatest service to our realm by keeping you company here'. 'But sir...', Daedalus was beginning to protest when the king roared, 'enough, the decision has been concluded. I will entertain no arguments'.

Daedalus, like so many freedom fighters was extremely demoralized and dampened and began to think that there was no light at the end of the tunnel. He turned to his son Icarus and began to explain to him that there was nothing to be done about it. But looking at the face of Icarus, he was forced to think that there must be something to do. Daedalus' heart was broken seeing his son in great despair and he took an oath that he would do everything in his power to make his boy a happy and fulfilled person. Daedalus, for the passing moment, stood tall watching the entrance of the cave which was overlooking the sea. He contemplated breakthrough. He watched the waves of the sea. The waves crushed on the rocks below and the seagulls circled over the cliffs. It was spring and the nests on the cliffs were filled with eggs and chicks. The contemplation of the father was extremely shaped when Icarus walked up beside him and cooed,

'How I envy those baby birds, for soon their wings be strong and they will be able to fly away from this wretched cliff'

Daedalus allowed a smile to form slowly on his gloomy face and turned to Icarus saying, 'well then, my little fledgling, we would best start working on strengthening your wings so you can be off with the others'. When a man something, the entire universe conspires in working it out. Daedalus began to use strips of leather and fine twigs to fashion a broom and a large net which he had Icarus dangle down towards the cliffs to sweep up the feathers near the seagull nests. Icarus continued to gather the feather for many days. Daedalus created thin tubes of light metal which he used to form the frame of two pairs of man-sized wings. He used leather strips to create a harness and pulleys to allow the wearer to flap and tilt the wings in various directions. After doing this, he took the feathers collected by Icarus together with the waxed candle to form and attach the feathers to the light metal frames. Icarus noticed the number of frames his father was building, and exclaimed with excitement,

'Two frames? Are you coming too?'

With the same excitement, the father retorted, 'I am, my son. Thank you for reminding me that of all my creations, you are the most important to me. I am sorry that it has taken me so long to free us both'.

They were ready to part way from the cave and the wicked king Minos. But first, he made extreme efforts to lecture the young lad on the flying venture,

'Now my son, remember, you must be cautious when we fly. Fly too close to the ocean and your wings will become too heavy with the water that sprays off the waves. Fly too close to the sun and the wax will melt and you will lose feathers. Follow my path closely and you will be fine'.

Icarus agreed with his father. But it seemed his excitement overwhelmed him tremendously. He listened absently when his father explained the cautions and tactics for a successful flight and how to use the pulleys to steer. After the lecture, it was time for departure. Icarus soared so high and higher aided extremely by the wind that had caught his wings as if it had been waiting for him all this while. Icarus felt for the first time the taste of freedom. He threw his head back and made mockery of the seagulls which stayed away from him and then swooped back squawking warnings when he got close to the nesting cliffs.

As Icarus continued to fly and to enjoy a high height, the father cautioned him again and again. He asked him to be careful and stop playing with the birds and follow him toward the shore of an island in the distance. But Icarus was overwhelmed with too much fun. He threw all his father's cautions to the wind. He was tired of continually following after his father, tired of his endless boring lectures. He was bored by his talks on carefulness. He watched the seagulls rise on the air currents high up over the sea. He followed after the free birds without calculating the level of his own freedom. He wondered and marveled at the height of freedom he enjoyed which he never knew about since he was in that cold damp cave for many years. He continued to follow the seagulls up and up and up into the sky. He could not resist the temptation. The father shouted again,

'No Icarus, stop. The wax will melt if it gets too warm. Not so high. Not so high!'

But if only Icarus had listened. The father was busy talking to himself. His audience was not interested. Icarus did not listen. He was lost in his own happy thoughts and excitements and ignored the father. Finding himself at a higher height, he began to feel the warm wax dripping down his arms and the feathers started falling out like snowflakes all around him. He remembered his father's caution. But of what need was it crying when the head was already off? Of what good was it making medicine for the dead? He began to work the pulleys to tilt his wings back down toward the sea but as he did so, he saw more feathers drift away and he began to lose height more quickly than he had thought.

Daedalus watched in extreme grief. He was helpless. Icarus made all frantic efforts to assuage the tragic situation but it was all to no avails. Finally, he had hit the rock. There were no feathers remaining. Daedalus followed as quick as he could where his son had fallen but the only sign of his poor child was a few feathers floating in the waves. He mourned his son so bitterly. He wanted many times to blame his escape from the king in the first place. But he managed to stay undeterred and educated himself that death in free land was more than life or any enjoyment, glory and pleasure in captivity and bondage. He renamed the island Icaria in memory of his dear son. He also erected a temple to the sun god Apollo.

'Do you wish to end up like the Icarus?' The father of Obi posed after his story.

'No, I do not want to, Dad'. Obi responded like an angel, so calm and recollected like one who has been showered with cold ice water. He had been keenly following the narrative by his father. He was extremely enthralled.

'You know you are just sixteen years old. It was the same age Icarus was when he got himself destroyed. Do not destroy your own self, son.'

Deeply touched by the tale, Obi made up his mind to turn a new leaf, to become a different and better person. He has suddenly transformed. Such was the thought of his father, so he judged. So he (Obi) portrayed and communicated in words and countenance. So much for the popular Greek tale! Obi promised to lead a better lifestyle. He promised change after learning the Greek tale. At this juncture, the hilarious father amused the atmosphere the more.

'I am certain this is not APC kind of change?'

For the passing moment, the father and son stayed long in the outburst of laughter, amusing each other until they arrived the school. For the very first time throughout the morning, they enjoyed this amusing moment.

'No, it is no APC kind of change. But do you really have some issue with APC? I suspect you; you are a PDP'

'No, I am not either. There is essentially no difference between the two. They are just one thing existing under different names. I am strictly nonpartisan yet not apolitical. Politics is good but has unfortunately been abused. Politics permeates all our lives but it is saddening and heartbroken how so little most people particularly under the guise of faith or religion have come to demonstrate their ignorance and dastard indifference and sheer negligence towards government. They abandon politics to the bad members of the society and they suffer the bad leadership. Sad enough, they fail woefully to understand that religion itself is the biggest politics'.

'Dad, please don't scandalize me. I am still a boy. By the way, our history teacher told us in the class last week that religion and business are two ends of the same snake. Is this the same thing you mean? I mean, how correct is our best hailed historian?'

'Obi', the father tenderly called him understanding that he had said more than the child could chew, more than was needed, 'I did not mean to say all that my son. It was a slip of tongue. I was too amused with your new conversion or change of heart. Your teacher or so-called historian is not a believer; don't listen to him. By the way, come and get into your class; it is time for class. And pay attention while you are in the class. No truancy of any such'. Obi obliged. No more agitation. But deep inside him, the protest and polemic persisted; he did not stop telling himself that the best truth is uttered without knowing it, without noticing it, without dutifully preparing and engaging in it. Unselfconsciousness.

Not only the father but the entire family of Edoga surely did not want Obi to be destroyed like Icarus in a reckless adventure. Nobody wanted his doom. It was chiefly the cause for the family morning assembly following the Morning Prayer session. To deliberate on the kind of youth Obi was gradually turning into. But the genuine efforts to saving Obi would not be at the detriment of his early exposure, his own adventure and his Age. His early exposure was not negotiable and could not be compromised with any fears, so argued out by his eloquent uncle who insisted that Obi must fly. Obi's 'flying' was paramount. And he could not 'fly' without technology, without modern gadgets. All those who must go far in life must embrace and welcome the technology for flight and for freedom. It was the magnificent Age of gadgets. But the fears of the family rested ultimately on losing Obi in the course of his flying and adventure. It was a difficult decision for the entire house. If he flies, he has the wind of pleasure and excitements and intoxication to contend with. And the lad was already showing a very poor performance and result with his adventure with modern technology, with phone gadgets which necessitated for the second family conference in the morning. If, on the hand, he does not fly, he would remain in the cave like Daedalus and Icarus forever lavishing his potentials and his future. It was the cave of shallow exposure, incompetence, complacency, mediocrity, ignorance, delayed and denied education. Obi, despite his misdemeanor and punishment for the act, was not going to miss out from the school of the Age he lived in, from the academy of gadgets and learning, information and communication. All were willing and committed to finding a lasting solution to the threat, a healthier and more constructive solution. All was put into place to see to it that the house returned to and experienced her old lively home and fraternal joys again. Everyone obliged.

THE MYTH

3

It is said that looking at the lips of a king; no one would imagine that he sucked his mother's breast. Looking at Edoga today, many would not understand what it had been through, the long walk to maximal breakthrough and success both material and otherwise. And the family was not certainly going to sacrifice this hard-earned fame and ruin everything they have worked for over the decades for any perceived threat; for the very thing hanging around their neck; for the endangering lifestyle of the boy Obi. .Even so, their long years of tribulations and travails strengthened them to know better that the present threat was not insurmountable.

All the people of the community were conversant with the story of the family: of dogged struggles, hard-work, pains and rise to prosperity. Edoga has become a large family residence in Asaba, Nigeria and was represented traditionally with the lion image. In that ancient legend, members of the family never harmed or killed a lion and the lion had also kept its own part of the covenant; a lion had never hurt them. Even so, many people have criticized the clan as notorious for their cunny nature for choosing a lion for their totem because lion is seldom at sight let alone having it killed. People could exhaust all their life time on earth without having to see a lion except in the zoo or books or television.

A very popular legend about the Edoga's house was called the dance of the lion. It was a very special feast for the family. It was not held every time, every year and not even every five years. It was organized after every decade. During the great feast of the lion dance, all members of the family danced round the large compound of Edoga with lion in their middle, alive and roaring. The feast was for connecting deeper with all sons and daughters of the lineage. It was for family bonding. It was for strengthening their sacred covenant. The unrivalled sacredness for the beast of the forest, for the king of jungle, for lion.

The mystical feast was also for family cleansing. Hence, it was called the holy feast of lion dance or family cleansing or purification. Any traitors in the family or/and those who had committed heinous offences such as murder, human rituals, rape, incest, idolatry and shown serious deviation from the family root, from the original tradition of their forebears were readily singled out and devoured by the fierce lion. For this, all members were gravely obliged to make their appearance without playing truancy or avoidance game. In some serious cases, it was related that the lion had covered long distances to bring defaulters back home before feeding on them. Yet, no one was certain about this tale. It was rather alleged that it was the lion of the tribe of Judah (Jesus Christ) that was being alluded to according to some tradition.

The Edoga family has grown in number, learning, nobility, strength, affluence and wisdom. It has grown relatively so large and so affluent from poverty and dishonors; from countless difficult times and sufferings. For one thing, the tale of the family and lion has helped tremendously to shape and define the general morality, decency and integrity of all the members of the family - mindful or fearful of what awaited them if they engaged and indulged themselves in any conducts that discredited the family name and undermined their hallowed original identity and reputation. At the moment which the threatening and endangering lifestyle of Obi was jeopardizing the family image, many stood to question if truly the boy was fully aware of the consequence of his actions; if truly he understood the old long tradition. The dance of the lion. Or it was the case that he had chosen blatantly to lose his life to the fierce and devouring lion as a feasting meal?

At the very gigantic silver gate of the family, there were no intimidating inscriptions and impressions such as 'Beware of dog' or any of the categories associated with the bourgeois of the society. Rather, there was a bold brief and modest inscription running on both sides of the entry gate, **'EDOGA IS IN THE HAND OF GOD'.**

LOOSE CHILD

4

Saturday,

6:00

Morning Devotion

It was quite a loving chill morning. Family morning Assembly and devotion usually commenced at five-thirty in the early hour of the day except on weekends and holidays. This was to enable those going to work and school to have quality time to do so and avoid lateness to functions. The prayers went on for a considerable time beginning with songs and praises. All members of the family were frequently present at the gathering. At worst, some might step in a bit late having passed added time negotiating with their bed and early morning slumber. Obi was a leader in this category. He was notorious for lateness to prayers. But even at that, the late comers still had something to boast of. They were still able to meet up with some aspect of the prayers. The usual lengthy prayer helped late comers to still participate without missing out from the blessings completely.

Today was also the feast day of the great saint Patrick who the family had special fondness for. He was a fifth century missionary born in Britain and was taken to Ireland as a slave after he was gruesomely kidnapped at the young age of sixteen. Readings and prayers about the saint were duly observed. Saint Patrick has occupied a very large space in the history of Christianity and evangelism of Ireland where he returned to convert it after his miraculous escape from slavery. And he was long also proclaimed and inaugurated the (second) patron saint of Nigeria, after the Blessed Virgin Mary. He was also well inaugurated and enthroned and enshrined in the Edoga's family, if not for anything else, the saint was the name sake and patron Saint of Obi's father.

The Scot by birth whose right origin was Italy, hung in a colossal portrait between the linking passage and the living room. The special day of the consecration and enthronement of the saint's altar was superb and elaborately celebrated by friends, family and church members. The presider of the exercise that day was Reverend Father Ejike Godwin.

The event raised some suspicions and rumours across the town. It was perceived that the Blessed Sacrament was being installed in Edoga's house as it has become a practice with many wealthy parishioners found in the habit of controlling the church and priests to the extent of privatising the Holy Eucharist and erecting the tabernacle in their private homes. They buy over the priests, the Eucharist and the church. They did this and more with high impunity, without the least regards for the sacred. But all the suspicions and rumours lacked substance. It was not true. The truth rather was that it was the memorable day the great Saint Patrick was being enthroned in the house of Edoga, not the Blessed Sacrament as erroneously perceived.

There were other Catholic emblems as well as the photos of the members of the family suspended at different strategic corners and angles. Obi's parents' enlarged wedding photo faced boldly the entire colossal interior space taking a chunk of the space on the wall. There were also photos of the children and individual photos marking certain remarkable events. Among the cross section of the photos was Obi as a new born baby and his just celebrated sixteenth year birthday. Very close to Obi's photo was the saint in the portrait dressed in his bishopric MITRE, crosier, staff, as well as the image of a snake. One of the popular tales of the saint was that he controlled and sent all the snakes at the Ireland into the sea while he was at prayer. Understanding this aspect of the life of the saint had always been quite problematic for the teenager. Each time he gazed at his own photo, he looked at the saint with certain misgiving. It has not helped in any way to give a good image of him before his pious father, before the entire family, before many others. Obi has stayed long in the habit of always coming close to the emblem or sometimes from a distance and staring it. Whenever he gaped at the saint, seeing the companion snake emblem, he always doubted and dismissed the tale as a myth. One fateful day when he was just at it again, one of his uncles walked into the house and they had some quick exchange.

'Good evening uncle, my dad just wanted to invite you over; he is in need of seeing you. He said network has been bad and he has not been able to connect to you.'

'Good evening, I am here now to see him, how are you Obi?

'I am alright, just that I am troubled a bit by what I see here.'

'And what is that? No, you should not be troubled. He is a great saint and great one to the house. The account of his works and wonders are overwhelming and known all the corners of the earth.'

'Exactly, what the problem is all about; I am thinking about those wonders.'

'Well, I am impressed you do. He can work any wonders you so desire in your life. We have long waited for miracle in your life. I am even more impressed now with your admiration of the saint. You both have something in common.'

'And what is that, uncle?'

'His heroic life started at childhood when he got kidnapped to Ireland but he later escaped and became a great missionary'

'But what are you really insinuating uncle; that I will also be kidnapped? God forbid it.'

'God forbid it too, my dear Obi. But that is not really what I am saying. Don't take my statement literally.'

'So, what are you saying then? Make yourself clearer.' Obi was unknowingly becoming rash.

'We all know you Obi, we are your family. And we all want the best for you. It is our hope and expectation that one day, God will kidnap you too for himself, but it is not the kidnapping you know. This one is a spiritual kidnap, a kidnap from your mundane and vain ways of life to the way of God, the purpose driven and productive way; a kidnap from vanity and futility of life to decency, virtues and Godliness. You ought to pray fervently for that. You must have to be kidnapped by God. Or do you prefer the lion to do it, to devour you into parts for your ill-conducts? That will be extremely disastrous. You will not be alive to tell the story'

'Thank you so much for that. I take that for a compliment. Anyway, uncle, don't tell me you believe that fairy tale about the dance of the lion. Uncle, you are far smarter than that. I know you are kidding me. It was just one of the traditions concocted in order to impart morals and help keep the family free from reckless and evil people. To put fear into people and help them live rightly. No lions anywhere, no dance of the lion'

'So are you, Obi – irresponsible and wayward. The tradition should in like manner help to re-amend and recondition your life for good'

'Anyway, Uncle, there is something that has seriously caught my attention as I was saying moment ago.'

'Speak my boy.'

'Come to think about it, how true is the story of Saint Patrick and the snakes? Did it ever happen, how true or legendary is the popular account? I fear to say that I find myself beset by so many doubts. I judge it to be in the family with the account of the famous and glorious dance of the lion'

'This is why I said a moment ago that we pray for your total redemption. But I did not know that you have degenerated to questioning and challenging the sacred.'

'Uncle, you know we are still in the mood of the great season of Easter. Give me some accolades please and not all these accusations and stereotypes. At least, it is holy week.'

'Well, all I know is that the story is true. The Church does not teach what it is not true. By the way, if you feel interested, read Jocelyn Furness' account and you will find much corroboration for what I am telling you.'

'Yes, I know about Jocelyn's writing. Read Monaghan and you may be shocked to learn that there were no snakes in the Ireland let alone to drive them away. This is for the simple reason that the snakes couldn't get there because the climate was not favourable for them. The reptiles could have only arrived the Ireland just ten centuries ago, and that was many centuries after the death of the glorious saint.'

'I see you have eventually started to read...' The uncle remarked and commended sarcastically.

'Yes uncle...Dad asked me to do so; he said that readers are leaders.' Obi was momentarily and greatly excited without properly interpreting the Greek offer.

'Ok, your Dad has done well in transforming your reading culture. But he certainly did not ask you to indulge in notorious sources or books.'

'But uncle, who says that they are notorious, who defines, validates and canonizes them? This is how we receive and swallow so many ideas and teachings that lack even the least approximation to the truth and we have lived with them for so long that they cannot be challenged or changed.'

Obi was still speaking when his father dashed out of his room to welcome his brother and drove Obi inside.

'Get inside this kid, I did not ask you to read antichrist. I can now bet with my whole life that this is how exactly you also misquoted and misrepresented your history teacher saying what he never intended'

Inside the house that day many years ago before Obi started his college education, Obi's father and uncle discussed at length about Obi's disposition to the church teachings. Yet, the uncle has visited that the day to discuss something else of immerse importance. It was about the painful encounter of Obi's uncle that day. The uncle had driven out of the house since in the morning in an elegant look and returned troubled, with heart break. He had been onto something for the most part of the year. He graduated from one of the best universities in Nigeria and was the best graduating student. He started his Doctorate degree programme. Academic politics, however, intervened and a committee of faculty and professors voted against giving him a doctorate degree chiefly because of his young age, intimidating intelligence among others. Despite the fact that he stood the best person for the job and position he aimed for in the institution, he was not considered just because of his very young age that intimidated other aged and elderly professors who did not want the young man. He yelled and groaned in pains:

'Fears and wickedness have crippled our people from allowing positive change through the youth. Obsessive fear has made them too protective, insensitive and destructive; envious and malicious.'

Obi's father listened patiently and passionately to his brother's story. He did well to console and motivate him. With the connection and the good name of the family, he was willing and ready to pursue his brother's ambition to the logical conclusion. Or better still, if not necessarily in that institution, there were other places that would gladly want to have his genius brother. But his brother was equally beginning to think and consider something else - to leave the country. He would continue with his post graduate studies there. Obi's father also welcomed this idea. But first they prayed about it. It eventually became the best option for the family, for Obi's uncle. Abroad, his age was not undermined. He was not treated by his age but competence.

The usual lengthy prayer and family devotion had some colouration with the popular prayer of Saint Patrick. A long prayer session that inwardly did not settle well with some other members of the family beginning with Obi the chief antagonist. Some still dozed off during the prayer sessions, not only at night, but even in the morning. It was best to always have all eyes well closed. This was because, most of the awkward positions and body posture of the members could trigger serious and lasting distractions. It was always common with the granny in the house.

Sometimes, her situation was understandable by everyone given her advanced age. But she did not get this understanding all the times. Other times, her son scolded and rebuked her as though she was a baby for always sleeping off during prayers and indulging in what only the heathens and infidel would do. She always forgot that the devil had been moving and roaming about looking for who to attack and possess and deceive since the old days of Eden and Job. At such occasions, the pious son usually spiritualized the entire content and warned her intensely of the pranks and tools of the devil possessing and using her. He never stopped reminding her of the wandering devil in the Eden and Job's household looking for who to demolish.

But the message or spiritual counselling session that was usually full of reprimands was useful only to one listening; granny did not care at all. The poor old woman oftentimes nodded head in different directions almost falling off from her sitting position. 'One day, you will land so terribly on the floor and crash your body…' Her daughter in-law once teased. But she never minded. She did not care a bit. She would rather defend insistently and made the moment a very amusing atmosphere for all who were present, 'If I fall down, you will carry me up; that is why I married you.'

But no time had been as hilarious as the different dramatic occasions, the little granddaughter ran up to give her some slap at the shoulder, back and different parts of the body during prayers to bring her back to consciousness. It was this child's drama that encouraged essentially the rule and habit of closing of eyes to control distractions, for the avoidance of the devil. But it was never a lasting remedy. The other part of the dramas involved the usual annotations rendered by the granny intervening in prayers and readings. While the person leading the prayer said the intercessory prayer, read and explained the scriptural passage, she intervened with recurring and amusing comments.

At a particular point, the leader was at it again asking petition for all those who were sick and for healing. He challenged God with the biblical injunction that says that human body shall not be an abode for infirmities and diseases. Her remark quickly came in as usual, 'So, it is written…but sickness has refused to listen, rather it has come and taken occupation of man in the head, hand, stomach, leg… just have a look at my leg, I cannot walk properly… chest and all parts of the body…seriously, we don't know who wrote all those things.' Prayer was paused for the passing moment. All stared at her. All of them were seriously amused as usual. Everyone knew how too long her leg has troubled her and conditioned her practically in one place always sitting and lying down for very long times.

Somehow, some members of the family have represented their candid view concerning the usual lengthy prayer in the house. They thought that the efficacy of prayer must not be predicated on its length, long recitations or verbosity. But the father and mother who were still basking in the euphoria of their born again, new life in Christ and life in spirit would never consider or heed to such an anti-prayer and an approximate demonic intervention. 'Even the good Lord and master recommended and gave humanity the best modest prayer session ever, the 'Our Father' and cautioned against the use of many words and wanting to impress at prayer. But man in the position and capacity of the spiritual leaders chose to overlap, overlay and belabour it.' Obi, the perceived deviant son, had carefully observed and boldly remarked at one occasion.

But Obi was no one in the house to be taken seriously. He was approximately a nobody when it was faith and morality. He was one whose opinion regarding prayer was not reckoned with. He was totally inconsequential when it was matter of spirituality. He was obviously the black sheep in the house. He was the Judah existing among the twelve. Obi was speedily and inconceivably growing horns and going naughty and notorious. In fact, it was for his sole matter that the usual morning assembly stood out quite uniquely and took a completely different dimension. Special session was on immediately after the Morning Prayer to treat and deal with the trouble he was making, his moral recklessness.

The granny noted while opening the adjudication process, 'our people say that one palm fruit does not get lost in the fire. 'Everyone understood her very perfectly. Obi could not be allowed to waste just like that. He was the only son among many girls. Even if he was already lost, he was going to be found. All hands were on desk. Another family session opened just immediately to deliberate and adjudicate on Obi's endangering character and general lifestyle. His redemption was ultimate.

SPARING FATHER, SPENDING SON

5

Monday

7:00

He was practically unobserving and oblivious of his surroundings. Not the sounds that came from the cars, the bellow of the horns, the whispers, talks and sounds of people all over, walking the street and carrying out different activities. Not the sight of numerous vehicles, structures, people and other things surrounding him like the numerous dramas by the roadside and inside the vehicle. Not the fine morning smell, the early morning good scent, the smell from the market pathway he had to pass through, the aroma of different food preparations and catteries around the town, the stinking ordour from the rough and messy gutters, bad drainage, different landfills and dumps and littered places he sometimes found himself as he walked. Even the early morning drizzling that dropped on him made no impressions either. He was completely all to himself in his lone thought.

It was Obi's father many years ago attending to a very serious mission, almost a journey of life or death. He had so much to lose if he failed in the mission and so much to gain from the success of the journey. He was called Patrick but Pat for short. This was the reason the devotion to Saint Patrick was accorded more fervour. He was on a fast pace when he was not on a vehicle. And even when he was inside the vehicle, he felt sometimes it was not moving as fast as he wanted it. People saw him almost standing in the vehicle as though his standing would add anything to the acceleration of the vehicle. But he was almost unaware of all this. Only one thing filled his mind.

Pat walked with so much haste totally unobserving and unconscious of many things because he was late to the job invitation and interview he was messaged to participate two days ago. The invitation simply read: 'We are happy to let you know that you have been shortlisted for our company job interview after receiving your request last week. Let us know if you will be there or not. Thank you. Punctuality is the key. Be early. Be smart.'

The only thing in Pat's mind was the job. The interview. Nothing else. He had received that short message early in the morning of Friday, March, 2000. The address was also given in the message. That was the first week after his POP (Passing Out Parade) from the National Youth Service Corps (NYSC). Pat was in the job market like so many other people, so many other unemployed graduates and youth in the country. Unemployment was everywhere and nothing to write home about with the teaming population of the country. It had resulted and led to so many different social ills, criminalities and nuisances all over the places. The connoisseurs, social scientists and experts were sensitizing the populace about population explosions and its attendant ills, evils, and negative consequence. The experts were at it again wedging wars against population explosion as if it was the worst plague, the worst heresy.

But to the Holy Church, it was rather some of the unorthodox and uncanonized measures and ways the scientists have adopted over times that were heretical. But virtually everyone understood that unemployment was among one of the dangerous outcomes of overpopulation seriously endangering the society and the people all over. The experts could not just overlook it for any acclaimed piety, ethics and theology.

The government was perceived so much as not doing enough or anything to ameliorate and abate the already precarious situation. It was a time most people considered education and spending time, money and energy going to school as a complete waste. This was because jobs were so hard, if not impossible, to come by after graduation. *Who school help?* That was a very common and popular slogan also misleading the generality of the youth. Hence, for everything, Pat ought to take the bull by the horn, do everything within his power not to play around with the one-time opportunity of securing employment just almost immediately after his national service.

Pat, like other concerned citizens had had ample time to ponder and assess the possible causes of unemployment in the country. So many people put the blames on the government for lack of job provision and employment for her teaming energetic population. For these people, the strength of any nations rested on their youth who should be given due priority and taken into due plans and cares. Others blame it on the general educational system that produced half-baked graduates and citizens without corresponding skills and capacity building that would make graduates marketable and employable and also be producers and employers of jobs themselves. The western education was spotted to be limiting and unsatisfactory like the colonial education and had to be revisited and restructured to suit the present needs. For these individuals, the educational system was too theoretical and paper work without much practical and application of what were done in the universities and schools. Even science-oriented disciplines and professions suffered the same fate and were quickly collapsing due to lack or dearth of apparati, facilities, research, experimentations and practical applications of the numerous classroom readings and talking. Yet, for another party, the blame was more on the individuals and citizens who should have learnt to think outside the box to give themselves generously to acquiring skills, trades and becoming self-employed, self-reliant and also employers of jobs. It was a time skill acquisition was trending everywhere and everyone's status was reading 'self-employed'.

But for Pat, when he had the time to ponder on this, it was neither the first nor the second nor the third reason but the three collectively put together that were the plausible causes of the ravaging problem of unemployment and hunt for jobs. The government, educational institutions and individuals were not exempted, and particularly the government which has assumed the role of a father to take up the responsibility of providing for his children.

But ultimately, Pat was not thinking of all this. If he ever did, it was certainly not at this moment. His mind was completely blank except for the job preoccupying him; his mind running continuously on where possibly questions could come out and how to perform exceedingly well in the interview. When he remembered the job, he was elated. He jumped in euphoria of excitement. He smiled to himself tacitly. 'Let this job work out for me. O God, help me.' He had prayed earnestly and frequently as he journeyed that morning. His level of recollection and indifference to his surroundings was so high that he could remember and think of them only after he was done with the interview.

Inside the vehicle, one of the passengers picked a serious quarrel with the driver. The disagreement went on for a while. The passenger just after few minutes of boarding the vehicle, received a call from someone and wanted to discontinue the journey. But she had made his payment. And that was where the contention lay. The passenger asked for the refund of his fare, even if it were a half of it. But the driver was not yielding to it. No refund of money after payment.

Rebecca was the name of the passenger. Rebecca was hard working, intelligent and beautiful. She was heading to her work place this morning but she has left at home an important file she had worked through the night. Rebecca was full of life. She had her strengths and her lights too. She was outspoken. And it has tremendously helped her this morning. Yet, like it is true with all human beings, she did not have it all. A singular shadow and dark part of her seemed to have written off all her good and positives. Nobody in the world was as scared to go into relationship as Rebecca. Nobody in the world was fearful to fall in love as Rebecca. When discussion was raised around the area of her relationship, if ever she allowed it, she always filled her listener with plethora of reasons why staying all alone to herself was the best choice she had made and nobody could make her to do otherwise. Those reasons usually revolved around heartbreaks and broken relationship, and Rebecca has actually had one or two of it. Those friends had told her those many times that she could count herself fortunate and favored for there were those who had had her experience countless times, yet they still said yes to love, they still welcomed relationship. Still, her reasons revolved around trust, trusting men. It revolved around the fear of the unknown.

There was on the other hand, those who viewed her experience from the perspective of karma. It was said that this group of people were probably too harsh and unfair to her. But no one knew exactly the truth. Yet, what happened that day in her life was well known by many who were not close to her. She was enjoying a day full of thrills in a chat with a friend she had met online over a month until they opted to do a call. She dropped her contact number in the chat. He also dropped his. It was at this point that the trouble kick-started. She asked him, 'so, I should call you? So *funni*indeed'. He was turned off immediately. He wanted calling her but was terribly disillusioned and he gave up calling her again. After some quiet moment, he retweeted,

I am shocked at your interpretation, lady. Primarily, what happened was exchange of contacts. When contacts are exchanged, they are saved up so that the caller will not have unknown identity during call, and will have less to say for introduction. But unfortunately, you chose to interpret it your own way. This is a typical (Nigerian) women's mindset. It is simplistic, closed, narrowed, narcissistic and too poor. Let me agree with your interpretation for a while: Why will you find a problem calling but do not find the same problem if I call you? The only valid answer is playing woman card rooted in timidity and self-absorption. Sincerely, your interpretation turned me off. Something I was not even thinking about. Yet, thank you immensely for letting me know the kind of person you truly are, the kind of persons some ladies are. You belong certainly to the category that do not promote mutuality and reciprocity in relationship but entitlement.

It was the end of the road between Miss Rebecca and her social media friend. Some said that the young man was the best husband Rebecca never married. They said that opportunity comes but once. And she did not make efforts or took some steps to amend what she damaged in her quite promising relationship. So, the man was the best husband she missed the chance of marrying and karma has caught up with her with the numerous other toasters and men that only came and broke her heart and left her in endless search for the right person. People said that Rebecca was like so many women and people who judged it is abomination for ladies to call a man, talk to a man, approach a man and decently express themselves but paradoxically the same ladies found nothing wrong approaching and talking to wrong channels, wrong people like the native doctors, pastors, numerous spiritual centers and prayer houses where they do terrible things seeking for men/husband but failed to do the basic. This new group of cultural revolt blamed it so much on a culture and tradition that make women secretive and manipulative but not expressive and assertive enough to their human concerns and needs. They belong to a group of social reform, paradigm shift and repositioning the compass of the society.

Eventually, there was some intervention from the other passengers and there was a bit of reconsideration resulting to the change of mind of the driver to remit part of the money to Rebecca after a long time of wailing. In the long run, her outspoken nature paid off. She did not have the phobia for talking and talking out. But Pat's attention was not really there. His mind was far away from where his feet were. He only bothered rather for the time. A lengthier drama that should have moved the job candidate was the early morning preacher inside the vehicle who spoke with every might and strength on top of his voice. He was skinny a man, average height and wore mismatching suit trousers and suit jacket that could run his body size thrice! He was swimming in the amusing dress. Everyone stared curiously at him. But the preacher was a second indifferent fellow in the vehicle. He was not amused in the least. He did not give a damn of what impression they had about him.

With his sizable Bible, he was rather calling on the people for repentance and acceptance of Jesus as their personal Lord and Saviour. He did not see himself as a prosperity gospel preacher but one after their change of life and purity. Immorality was the heart of his message. The nucleus was fornication. Not many people inside the vehicle admired his message particularly the youths. But there was a side of the preacher they admired. Not just his funny look but also how he preached. The how despite the what, put virtually everyone rolling in under the anointing of laughter except for Pat. The indifferent Pat. The job candidate.

The preacher showed hidden obsession for short bum and rebuked and condemned sternly ladies who indulged in the act as well as other forms of nudities and sexual immorality. The loudest laughter came when he related a story of a girl who to his best of judgment was responsible for the untimely death of a certain fellow. He was distracted by her short bum, did not concentrate on the walkway and was crushed by a car while he stared sheepishly at the girl. The pastor cum preacher made an illustration: 'The girl rolled her bombom like ceiling fan. The poor boy stared and died for bombom he never benefited from'. The people were seriously thrilled by the poetic and dramatic presentation of his preaching. It was hard to tell whether it was a gospel message or some sort of entertainment comedy show. But in the end, much was achieved. It made the journey livelier and less serious for the passengers apart from Pat who was quite preoccupied with his interview.

Mr Ojobo was the name of the morning preacher. He was tall and light in complexion. He certainly had small body size yet his head seemed to be twice smaller than all the other parts of the body which always made him to look quite awkward and amusing. Inside the vehicle, not all the people knew him. Yet, a good number of the passengers remembered him for the regular bus preacher who presented his messages always with so much attendant dramas. Among these people, it was well believed that the work of a pastor was truly a call from God. They sometimes expressed it as 'who God has arrested no one could certainly bail the person out'. Yet, the arrest of Mr Ojobo by God was not from the traditional known sins, notoriety, atrocities, evils and wayward living like it were with ancestors such as saints Paul, Augustine, Matthew, Ignatius and many others in that long list. Leaving his own place or town to go to different places in order to spread the message of God was the greatest miracle people always shared to have happened to the pastor. For the pastor suffered chronic fear or phobia to move out of his comfort zone to any new places and unknown destinations. He had grown and had all his education in one single place and would still want to spend all his life in the same place without exploring other parts of the world. He did not bother a bit. And he has not bothered about many things in life. Like the flowing suit he was putting on this morning. With the pastor's experience, many people came to trust more in miracles.

When Pat was informed of the job interview, the message he received played good melody in his head again and again to a dancing comportment. He was fully alert. He was happy. It made his day. It made his entire weekend. Throughout the weekend, he took out quality time to prepare seriously and adequately for the forthcoming interview and subsequent employment. Preparation, it is said, is the key to success. He had heard that time and again especially since his formative years. It was time for him to show it in action. He needed to be in his best person and look good and presentable. He put so much time and efforts to realize the result. He had learnt in life that appearance is the first letter of recommendation and also, one is oftentimes addressed from the way the person dressed. He was not going to leave any stone unturned. He was certainly not going to leave anything to chances. He washed his cloths. He starched them. He ironed them properly, got his shoes and tie ready and handy. He prepared adequately for the interview. He gave it his best. But sometimes one's best was not always enough.

Four o'clock in the early hour of the morning, he was already up from the bed. He had hardly slept deep even for the other hours of the night. He was partly awake and partly asleep. First, it was because of his excitement for the job and second, the anxiety to wake up early to avoid going late to the interview. He had spent the entire weekend reading hard and making findings on the relevant tips and hints to making a successful interview and securing the job easily.

On arrival at the designated place, what Pat met at the premises shocked him beyond imagination. He saw haggard looking interviewers. He got a quick and sharp instinct that he had been scammed. But at least, he was consoled that apart from the time and preparation he invested in the exercise, he did not pay any money. So, for him, if it were truly a scam, it was minimal and manageable.

The offices where he had come to, looked hired, haggard and rowdy. They talked lousily and persuasively. The people made ostentatious claims that they had millions or they made millions in their business. Pat was well congratulated on getting a job before finally they came to tell him the truth of their identity. And it came only after a long while of persuasion and insistence from Pat. He was getting tired and speedily growing impatient of their long talks and motivational messages like cheap roadside preachers. At long last, they confessed to him that they were members of a multi-level marketing company.

Pat went white. He was weak. Every part of him was shut down. He hardly held and restrained himself from pounding anything around him. Immediately, he pulled out his tie and hid it in his long envelop. He only realized later how he yelled at them:

'This is deception. This is unacceptable. This is pure scam. You guys should stop manipulating people around or I get you all arrested for malice...'

He was yet speaking when another person interjected:

'Oga, calm down, just calm down. This one no be grammar matter. All these educated people without money…only big grammar but no money…. Just know for your information that education is nothing. Education is the real scam. So correct yourself first….na who school help?'

'I don't blame you. It is none of your faults. It is all mine. If only I did not come here. If only I did not bring myself here even under this rain, you would not have the effrontery to babble and talk trash. But I have no words to exchange with you rascals and charlatans. I have no time for you. All I say is before you continue to progress in your error, before you continue to expose and advertise your ignorance talking and attacking education, go and make sure you get enough education first. This is the Age of school. There is still a large room for you to learn even at this stage. Don't say no to adult education. You need it. Do good to kill the phobia you harbor about knowledge, learning. Or it will ruin you eventually, and that is if already you are not destroyed. Don't be repulsive and resistant to knowledge. It is brains the society seek not thwarts.'

Since after and even during the Morning Prayer, just before the second session of the family meeting commenced, Pat was seriously engulfed in this flight of thought about his youthful days and experience at seeking for job, his old days of humble beginning. He had related the story many occasions in the house and all members of the family were conversant with the fascinating tale. Thinking about Obi's strange lifestyle has led him to remembering his past humble days, the old days of hard struggles. If only the little Obi knew the many years of hard-work that it took him to work himself through the ladder of success, taking all insults and submitting to many pains, he would behave himself.

Somehow, Mr Pat would not have much to worry about the expensive gadget possessed by his son Obi. Time has changed and his family has tremendously transformed from the old days of seeking for job to the new days of offering jobs; from the old days of having nothing to the present time where he has virtually everything any man/family could afford and boast of in life. Notwithstanding, for the modest, frugal and economy conscious Pat, it did not make sense but everything waste and stupidity to have a college boy carry with him such an expensive technology without him earning anything in life yet. It did not augur and tally with good economic principles for him.

Mr Pat's utmost belief and canon in life was that everyone must earn what s/he owns and spends. Anything other than this was stealing and criminality for Mr Pat. And spending and lifestyle of a wealth creator must be three layers below what and who s/he is. The entire community remembers Mr Pat for sharing with them, during one of his birthday celebrations, how if he found himself to pay certain big amount of money to sleep in a hotel, he would be awake for the entire night thinking he had been robbed in a broad daylight. Even the birthday anniversary, like his other celebrations, was not always elaborate, luxurious and proud. For he has been a strong critic of too much waste in the society, in the government and among people especially Africans' consumption syndrome that is manifest most times in unproductive and irrelevant ceremonies and celebrations. So it was related that he was walking the town the other day and hissed and groaned bitterly upon meeting a man who could barely feed two times in a day but the same man was busy making posters for the celebration of his birthday. He gave up on the reason and judgment of the people of his society when he heard that the man had to go borrowing just to make the celebration which had become a ritual that could not be avoided for any reason.

The story of the feasting man on one side of the equation and the judicious and frugal lifestyle of Mr Pat on the other side, people judged, corresponded perfectly to another popular or common paradox in the society where rich and well-to-do parents give birth to two or few children but poor parents and wretched families give birth in dozens. Part of what Pat had also shared with his community was not spoiling his children with affluent life – cars, wears and things they could not afford themselves. Mr Pat always blamed and wept for the economy of a society and a people who possess such false notion of life and false notion of wealth that everything must be paid, bought and expensive instead of producing and doing most of the tasks paid and spent on and cutting down consumption and capital consumerism at that. His bitterest wailing in the society was people living a lifestyle that they cannot afford, or better still, afford at least twice or thrice.

It was not surprising that Mr Pat earned from the public different cognomens such as stingy man, *aka gum* and others in that category. He was greatly chastised rather than cheered for his kind of economic principle, judicious and frugal lifestyle. But Mr Pat was not bothered even a bit. He was always dogged in his conviction and position provided he was not committing any crimes or breaking any laws of the society. The most memorable of all the stories of his judicious lifestyle was the day he attended a church programme for bazaar and fundraising. For Mr Pat was doubled also as a religious, Godly and God-fearing personality among other virtues. Some said that the bible especially many passages and injunctions on investments like the parable of three men given one, two and five talents differently; against wastage like Jesus' feeding of the crowd and asking them to pick up every leftover; judiciousness like the ten wise virgins and the parable of the steward have helped to shape and transform the lifestyle Mr Pat embodies and lives today.

That day at the church, unimaginable pressure, mental bullying, tortures, intimidation, coercion, duress and manipulation were leveled on Pat by the man of God for him to make donation like all others have done. But what the man of God did not know or he failed to understand was that Mr Pat never did anything or lived his life after others, following others or losing himself in others and in the world. His authentic life rooted and governed by freedom, choice and responsibility for progress and a better society forbade it. Mr Pat could only manifest his modest and judicious personality when he asked the pastor to prepare his budget for the church project and he would make his own commitment. But what Pat said seemed to have fallen on deaf ears while the extortionist in the guise and affidavit of man of God continued ranting and bullying the gentleman into a forceful decision. To the judgment of many, utmost equanimity, serenity, composure, comportment, calmness and control were exercised that day by Mr Pat who was not distracted and perturbed by the long bully and violations.

Before his long thought was cut short by the attention and deliberation of the family, he paused for a moment to imagine and try to unravel the happenstance between what was taking place in his very home and the news headline he was seeing online. It was about a teenage girl of about seventeen years old who had been held hostage in a supermarket phone gallery because the man that promised to buy her iPhone13 pro max had made away with the phone on excusing himself to make use of the convenience. It was indeed a black Tuesday for the poor girl. But Mr Pat's worry for her was the same with his own only son. His worry was not necessarily about the phone. But the gross greed, prodigality, extravagance, wastage, unreasonableness and irresponsibility that have engulfed the youths to aim and engage in what they cannot afford, to own what they cannot afford and to spend what they barely own. Nobody could really understand the mystery that explains the nexus between a sparing father as Mr Pat and a spending son as Obi. Or is it not rightly said that snake never gives birth to something short? All these questions remained unanswered regardless of Mr Pat's efforts and struggles to find answers just before the second conference began.

The family deliberation was just starting and quickly cut short his thinking. Everyone could see his long lonely thinking and the worry written clearly on his face. He was told and petted particularly by his wife to be calm, that everything would be fine. He listened. All was not totally lost. He rearranged and comported himself better for the meeting. The second assembly was on.

NARCISSUS

6

The second sitting was heralded by early morning rain. It had rained this way for the past days announcing the end of the raining season. The raining season started so belatedly due to climate change and many assumed that it was also going to add up some time before coming to an end. Those who thought that way wanted a compensation from nature. But that did not agree with science. The rain this morning came with much breeze and raised too much dust. Family members left to their various rooms to ensure the windows and louvers were well closed to stop not just the rain but ultimately the dusts from settling and resting on the furniture, bed and wears. When they resumed sitting, all were well seated in solemn mood and waited for Pat to open the discussion. Everything was about Obi.

Just celebrating his sixteen-year birthday, Obi's mind was far more mature than his real age. But there was a group that thought it was not maturity. It was purely dubiety. It was notoriety. Obi still had two years to finish his college education in Kings Memorial College but he did things beyond his age and class. Sincerely, Obi did not do so many things as a child which he was. He was generally not seen like other normal people. Obviously his charming look was far from normal.

At about quarter passed five o' clock on Monday when he was given birth to at the Annunciation Hospital, Asaba, the doctor had quickly suggested to call him Narcissus because of his charming look. He was called Narcissus but the name did not last long. The mother changed it almost immediately. After she carried out some finding on the name and figure Narcissus in ancient history, she disliked the name and did not want her son to die in the same way and manner the historical or mythical Narcissus ended up.

According to Greek mythology, after Narcissus was born, he was taken to a diviner to foretell what awaited the child, his destiny. The Oracle's prediction was not so good at all. The mother was told that the child would grow up not knowing who he was, and the very day he would come to that knowledge, he would die. And so it happened the day the Nymph, Echo, followed after Narcissus in irresistible admiration and infatuations of Narcissus' beauty. By the way, Echo had been cursed to be dumb by the goddess Juno for the former's garrulousness and loquaciousness. After refusing Echo's love advancement like he had done too to many others before her, Narcissus came to a water body where he was able to behold his own charming look. Gazing through the water body, he too got charmed to his own self until he perished without returning home. While in another context, he sat by the water so fixated until a god took pity upon him and transformed him into a flower. Since that day the meaning of Narcissus stuck – excess self-love, self-obsession, inflated self-importance, self-absorption, self-preoccupation. All this and more was what Obi's mother uncovered from her search and had her son's name changed to what it became today. Obi not Narcissus. But changing the name could not change the look. He was exceptionally good looking and charming. Changing the name also did not do so much (if any) to change the preoccupation, inflated importance and obsession with material cares and other cares Obi submerged himself and suffered just to satisfy himself and look big and expensive. Indeed, no one could change a fate. No one could keep appointment with fate. Hence, all his mother did to avert and abort the omen. It made her to tell her husband a certain night the oldest aphorism she got from her grandmother, 'you can feed the stomach as well as you could but it will still find something for itself without you knowing it'.

More often than not, the mother sat, knelt down or stood tall gazing up to heaven for her only son. She had always prayed so intensely that the good look of Obi could as well reflect in his darkened character. She had said that prayer many times and she was gradually getting weakened and giving up. But so much for the notable Catholic Saint Monica who in Christian history was known famously for praying her son Augustine out. Saint Monica has over times and across different situation become a source of inspiration and consolation for Obi's mother just like she has been to many mothers to pray without season; to keep praying and asking without relenting for their wards, for their children. One of the striking and curious parts of Monica's ordeal was the day Saint Ambrose saw her in pool of tears and exclaimed, 'Anyone who these tears are shed for cannot be lost.'

Ambrose for what it was did not lie. Augustine was saved from his extreme waywardness. Obi's mother too had had her hope reinvigorated at many different occasions from the stunning story of mother and son. Hardly could any child or son be as bad, spoilt and notorious as Augustine. She had prayed this way even more fervently this morning just before the commencement of the second assembly. But it was only the fruits of the conference that have demonstrated to her that the most part of prayer in life was achieved more in the quality of human interaction, action, communication, facing and accepting reality and doing the needful. Praxis was double prayer.

'Go get the nonsense phone, you this little demon, you will not kill me; I did not kill my own parents, so you will never succeed in terminating my life untimely.'

The father yelled with all his strength and might. Honestly, Mr Pat had suffered anger issue just as his own father and maybe grandfather too. It was a known ill running practically through the blood stream of the family including the females. It was a known fact that they all took it from their father. But Pat has been able to handle and curtail his own anger after encountering divine intervention many years in the past. It was a fascinating tale that eventually resulted to the sudden conversion of Pat to a born-again Christian. The day it happened, Pat almost killed someone out of his usual rage. It was a police man on the highway.

The police man had worked him up so bitterly with unnecessary checks and cross examinations which usually were pointing to something more – the shameless demands for money – enlightened exhortation of the people and whitewashed robbery of the public.

But after escaping narrowly the profile of a murderer, he returned home falling flat on the floor, and raising high his eyes to the heaven, he cried deeply and poured his heart out in supplication to heaven for God to cure him of the dangerous trait. His prayer was heard. It marked remarkably his divine conversion and the beginning of a new life.

Pat obtained his divine healing. But this morning his temper failed him again. His temper was so high. The emotion had not changed much despite the long Morning Prayer. But granny helped to stabilize his temper and calmed his nerves: 'No, that is not the way to proceed, it is wisdom not temper, prudence not muscles, brain not fist. Don't throw away the bowl with the baby. Do not cut off the finger with the nail. With prudence, we shall prevail and resolve everything amicably.'

'Listen to Mama my love', his wife cooed.

Finally, the truth was out. Obi could not keep his secret forever from the family especially his father. He dashed out of the room with one of the most expensive cell phones, iPhone 11 pro max. No one saw it coming. Everyone was bemused. The mother was dumbfounded. She was looking dazed and speechless but filled with unsettled thoughts, 'How did it happen; how did my son and only son for that matter get to this level of criminality? For certain, she knew too well that if she was to find good answer, it was certainly not to be in that troubled state, it was surely not in that disconcerted atmosphere.

Chill cold descended quickly on the house that usually ended prayer session in a very warmth atmosphere, dramatizing and relishing the amusement of granny in a lively session and mood. Today's morning was wide different. Everyone felt drain of blood in their faces and all parts of the body. What seemed to shock everyone the most was the level of elegance and boldness with which Obi walked and still carried himself even in the midst of the bedlam. He was the cause of the trouble, the early morning pandemonium. But he was never troubled. He was as calm and undisturbed as anything. His general outlook and comportment, obliged the father to accuse him more:

'Just look at him, he is so hard-boiled, toughened and indifferent, the best way to tell a notorious and impenitent criminal.'

Even granny could not stop or hold back the father at this moment. She too was beholding what drained her blood seriously with the endangering appearance of Obi. She irresistibly joined in the lamentation. She was not sure when she coughed out, 'When a madman runs the street, it is his people that cover their face in shame.'

Obi handed over the phone to the father. He went back to the seat. But the father ordered him to keep standing.

'I put it to you as your father to tell the entire house gathered here this morning who truly has this phone. Is this phone yours? Does it belong to anyone or you own it?'

'Yes, it is mine, the phone belongs to me'. Obi stammered but still possessed his stamina and equanimity.

'So now it is finally yours? It does not belong to your friend again? It is no more Bigger's phone given to you? You are going to pay dearly for this. I will get the cops to arrest you this morning. Oh, my father-God, you are so lucky that this is not the season of the great family feast, I would have you dance before the lion. I would have you devoured and eaten up by it. You will be so shocked at what I will do to you. You will wonder if I am truly your father that gave birth to you. Oh sorry, I have forgotten so easily. You seldom get shocked. But we shall see how it ends. This is getting out of hand. You cannot be living here in the house and be giving everyone fear of not knowing what would happen next. This is not your first time. This is not your second time. Everyone here knows it. You have stayed in this discrediting life for too long. Yesterday, it was jewelries. Today it is money. Tomorrow it will be phone. And so, it continues and no one can predict what next you are up to.'

It was moment after Pat was done talking that he could really realize how much emotion had taken toll on him. He realized too that he should not have said certain things. The invocation on the dance of the lion was not necessary. It was no longer in vogue. At least, not with the new path of life the family had taken against all others. By the way, was it not divinely written that those who choose other Gods increase their own sorrows? He too never believed in it, in the dance of the lion. At least not after his new life in Christ. Even so, Pat and the rest of the family had been confronted time and again by the eldest surviving member of the clan that Obi had been cursed by the land for the abandonment of the ancient family identity. The terrible and menacing lifestyle of Obi had been judged to have come from the Gods. And it would stay as long as when the house, particularly the father, was able and honest enough to face the reality, to face the truth to return to the root. Even at that, Pat had always answered that Christ is the truth. Christ is the root on which his life and the entire family is rooted. Christ is the new lion.

If only Obi had come out honestly to tell the father the truth at first, the situation would not have escalated this too bad. Rather than telling the truth, Obi had emboldened himself and his secretive path of life with dangerous questions. He had frequently asked himself the need for telling the truth, being truthful, being real or one's self without pretense and hypocrisy when the other (second) party was not wont and prepared to listen and behold the so-called honesty they preached. It made Obi to keep his true self only to himself knowing and understanding that the world he lived in was not ready for it. According to Obi, the world feared the truth; people are scared of the truth. So that when they preached the truth or asked one to be truthful, they were invariably demanding for falsehood and deceptions because the moment they know about the truth, they make their victims to feel bad, pains, ashamed, unloved, dejected and worthless. He ultimately saw telling the truth, being truthful and living a truthful life as a two-way thing. Not only the responsibility of the truth teller but also and even more importantly was the role of the environment in which the truth is demanded; there ought to be an appreciable level of openness and acceptance as different from the usual hostility and open hostility at that. Obi had not enjoyed a listening and tolerant environment. It was such openness that encouraged people to share themselves or things about their selves without living in secret. And vice versa. For the teenage boy, the father, family and environment he lived, had not been fearless and friendly enough to relate with him in the way and manner that would help him be truthful. He strongly accused his environment of not being open to truth which left him with no choice but false image. Obi believed that his environment forced him into the kind of lifestyle he lived today. Therefore, for far too long, Obi, stayed with false image. For about two weeks ago when the father noticed him with the ostentatious phone and asked after the ownership, Obi lied. He had told different lies to cover up his initial lie.

Blood is thicker than water, so it is said. The anger of his Mr Pat did not endure for long. Not so long. Again and again, the entire house spoke to him. They pleaded with him to tamper justice with mercy. It was difficult and took considerable length before calming the father down and making him to change his mind. Previously, he had passed his judgment that Obi was to be arrested and detained and punished. Obi had not only been guilty of owning such a property without anybody's knowledge but ultimately, he had lied blatantly and adamantly to the father and family time and again.

Have you ever heard that the father of all liars is the devil?' The father asked.

'No.' Obi denied it.

The father was vexed again. 'You are such a devil, you are a blatant liar', the father hurled.

The father listened to granny. Much after, he reconsidered his original judgment. But Obi was certainly not going to keep the property. The father's reason was three folds. The phone was too expensive for his person and age. It was judged that it could unnecessarily attract the bad guys and put him into serious danger. Closely allied to the above, he was to continue to make use of a smaller phone, Nokia 33 because he was yet too young to use an android smart phone. The third reason was glaring to everyone. It was designed to serve as a reprimand for the erring and recalcitrant boy. Virtually all members of the family concurred and were at home with the resolution and verdict. Everyone thanked and applauded the father for his wisdom and maturity in handling the matter. For the granny particularly, the father had done so well by not throwing away both the baby with the bowel. A good social distillation and distinction, granny acknowledged and exalted.

But there seemed to be only one person with a different opinion. It was Obi's uncle, who had recently returned home from Canada from his long years of studies and work. His view surrendering the verdict differed somewhat from the father. Both divergence and convergence of opinions were welcomed and duly looked into. In the end, it was the most refined and civilized of all the opinions. But it swayed and held a controversial, if not even an eccentric and deviant perspective.

PLAYING, DAMAGING AND BUILDING (DIVERSITY)

7

Obi's uncle was Ebube or Ebubechukwu in full. He was his paternal uncle. Obi was the favorite of nephews Ebube had. Yet, it would take long before the boy could come to realize this. Ebube had spent part of his educational life in Canada. In Canada, he rounded up his studies as a Computer Engineer. His dexterity and versatility with computer and machines was so impressive and outstanding. His best areas were cryptography, writing codes and encrypting programs as well as breaking of codes. Studying computer in school was something that did not take anyone who knew Ebube by surprise. It was something many had waited and always looked up to him for since a child. He appreciated the fact that his parents were not given to the traditional parental and perennial phobia in allowing children to explore and exploit their environments and technology. Since he was very tender, he was so given to playing a lot with computers. He kept so many of them as his toys as a child. He played with them. He worked on them. He damaged them. He did all this as a mock professional, practicing how he had always seen it done in movies and life when his father took him out to computer centers to buy computers or to fix up damaged ones. He did all this more because he had the enabling environment and space to do so both physically and mentally.

Physically, there were computers in the house as common household facilities and other places his father took him out to. Mentally, and this was even more important and enabling, the parents had a liberal mind and did not suffer from any fears, insecurity and restricting mindset that the child was yet too young for the gadgets and was only damaging properties. They saw beyond the play and damage. They understood he was already picking up something serious at that tender age. Machine and technology sense baked and shaped him as a child. High technological insights and mindset were already registering, making tremendous inroad and impacts in Ebube and building his entire person. At some level, the child was already dipped and deep in digital revolution. The parents especially the dad always admired, welcomed and celebrated such early induction and fought and resisted the contrary. The children's computers were always specially designed and protected with waterproof against easy damage and built as toys.

Ebube's father particularly had always counselled the mother to always allow children to familiarize themselves with company and environment that would induce and initiate and infuse knowledge and ideas. The company of gadgets and tools as well as great books the parents provided him aided tremendously to fire Ebube's imagination and reposition his learning and cognition and to ultimately redirect the compass of imagination and inventiveness. So, rather than just play with sand, stones, sticks, dirt and trashes that were unrewarding, wasteful and unproductive, the parents helped immensely to direct and tailor them towards more profiting objects and tools – gadgets and machines. Ebube's father oftentimes said, 'adults become what they eat, but children become what they play with'.

As a child, Ebube observed that there was in his father's house what he had not seen in other people's and friends' houses – a constructed separate apartment for computer room for children where they mostly spent quality time playing. They achieved two things doing one thing: they enjoyed themselves playing like other kids and invariably and unconsciously acquired so much exposure to gadgets and technological knowledge. Seeing the boy immersed in his routine play and how he was operating the device that day, the uncanny father summoned his dear wife and cooed,

'Look at him, watch him closely. Do you see the child? No, I know you don't see. You only see the body not the spirit. You see only the play, the objects and the damage. See his spirit is growing, forming and positioning. He is already learning and picking up valour, tools, technology, devices, determination, bravery, vigour and stamina. That is to say he is already feeding the spirit, the mind. The mind is already made and made early. That is how to tell a child that would go far, break new grounds, do wonders and make great exploits. Give a child space to play, fall, and damage and they will heal back but he will be a different person – strong, powerful and daring. Let them spoil things; let them cause damage at tender age. They will grow up great fixer of damages, fixers of problems. They will grow up not to be timid, idiot and indolent.

It was for his own interest and the interest of the nation that he returned from Canada after studies to practice professionally and contribute his wealth of knowledge, ideas and ingenuity to the motherland rather than contributing to building a foreign land as it has become so common and popular with so many African people which was carried out either in sheer ignorance or lack of patriotism for one's country or both. This is called, 'brain drain'.

His parents among others were particularly the key agitators for his return to Nigeria. He returned to the country despite the painful and lamentable experience he had had that culminated to his travelling out abroad. Nigeria needed him more than any others. To serve his father's land. He was largely seen and judged the best man for the job, the best man to address and rise to the occasion of innovations, productivity and total progress of the wasted and murdered nation and the total well-being of the good people regardless of the taunting and daunting challenge of the bad and corrupt system. So, his return to the country was apt and expedient. He returned to Nigeria early and quick after his studies in order to stop him from settling down lest it became too late.

But Ebube had already and gradually begun to settle down. He had found a lover of his life while in Canada for studies.

He did not go for a Nigerian girl. Not even a black girl. His soul mate was a tall, pretty, intelligent and striking Russian lady. Her name was Sophia. She studied optometry. A stunning and renowned physician. She was a polyglot too. She could speak six different languages fluently. The two were geniuses in their own right and capacities.

Deep down, Ebube knew and needed no angel to minister to him that he was treading a very difficult path with the choice of his marriage. He was raising a strong dust and he was going to have serious contest with the family, yet he was not discouraged and deterred, he proceeded for it. For one thing, Ebube had grown up to possess a mind of his own, a free thinker. One that contributed essentially to the trouble he had with the academic chair and professors while in Nigeria. The cultural mixture in his marriage was hard to be accepted. But he thought that it was certainly not insurmountable.

It was, however, this striking combination in his choice of marriage which many would ordinarily not admire and jump at but frown at and rebuke that actually intrigued and impressed Ebube the more and gave him more reason to consider the relationship. The uncanny, unconventional and controversial Ebube had always seen and defined marriage from the angle most people had not and will never dare to do. He had always admired and appreciated marriage contracted outside than within, and the further the distance both in geography and culture the better for him. He knew the level of phobia and insecurity people, more often than not, entertain in such marriage. Yet, he never saw it as insurmountable and impossible. Marrying and restricting marriage only and mostly to close and familiar environment and culture has led to a paper he called 'Marriage Has Defiled Mathematics Again: No Collection of Like Terms'

His position was simply that marriage is not mathematics where like terms are collected for solving equation. This is different from the question of compatibility and understanding. According to Ebube, uniformity and similarity do not define understanding and compatibility. He argued that majorly why gay marriage was discouraged in most societies was because it was a collection of the same sexes, a mixture of the same components, a product of the same compositions rather than different compositions as it is with the two popular genders, male and female, created by God to strike a balance. Yet, for him, most people were only able to see this homogeneity only in the sense of sex instead of spreading it across to other parameters and conditions too like culture and geography. *Why always prescribe marriage or fight and insist people must marry from the same country, the same state, the same town and even the same village as some do?* Ebube oftentimes asked. But he had never got an answer for that. Or what he always heard had never served him satisfactorily. For him, marriage should not only be a mixture of sexes but as well should be about a robust fusion of different geography and cultures cutting across any parts of the globe promoting integration, unification and trans-nationality. While abroad, he had given a lucid lecture on cultural diversity which he titled DIFFERENCE IS GOD'S GIFT OF INNOVATION. He illumined his audience that day in the following way:

'Diverse relationships matter, the more diverse relationships we have the less bigotry, the less intolerance, the less hatred, the less prejudice, the less racism in the world. This is because diverse relationships offer us all not just the benefits of a relationship but remarkably offers us a broad set of social experiences to draw from in forming our opinion of others and the world. Phobia is the first and strongest enemy of diverse relationship and why many people opt to remain only to themselves without exploring much. How do we connect with people whom we do not have anything in common with? Many people believe that the secret of establishing relationships with diverse group of people has everything to do with our ability to look past our differences and find things we have in common. I choose to reject such thinking on the basis that the statement 'look past our differences to find things we have in common' presupposes in my own humble intellectual summation, that there is something desirable about the things we have in common and something undesirable about the things we don't have in common. Elsewhere, I had taken time to point out to a friend who was lamentably complaining about finding life partner who shared commonalities like language amongst others, that marriage is unlike mathematics where like terms are collected but ultimately a union of two different individuals (not just sex or gender) coming together to accept, love and celebrate their differences. So, there is a paradigm shift. The thing of value is the thing that is different not necessarily the things we possessed in common. The secret to establishing a relationship with diverse group of people has everything to do with how we all perceive and respond to things that are different, different from us. But we have a choice here: we can perceive things that are different as things that are bad and threatening or we can perceive things that are different as things that are good and valuable. We can respond to things that are different by being uncomfortable, suspicious, doubtful, insecure and anxious or we can respond by being excited and curious. People see the world through different lenses: race, color, ethnicity, religion, political affiliations, social status, job, sexual orientation, sex, education and other boundaries. But the lens that should be most intriguing and most preferred for us should be the lens of a civilized mind equipped with the capacity for tidy thinking. Diverse relationships matter because they enrich our lives. They make us more sensitive. They make us more culturally aware and large. They make us larger than ourselves. They make us more compassionate and we don't have to have anything in common with people to connect with people, all we have to do is to be enthusiastic, be curious and embrace the idea that difference is good. Difference is God's gift of innovation. Last time I checked, the holy book never calls us to look exactly the same, function exactly the same or meet only those of our kinds. In fact, the body of Christ can only function as should when that doesn't happen – we must be different in order to fulfil all the various roles God has for us. Again, difference is God's gift of innovation. Marriage is no mathematics where we collect like terms to solve problems of life'

Ebube grew up sad to learn the level of people's mentality and entitlement to marrying only and mostly from familiar and immediate places and cultures usually their own very people and culture without mixing up adequately. The phobia to detach, leave home and go far. He enjoyed exogamy that crossed borders and boundaries of cultures to new frontiers in order to build bigger and stronger identities and species of humans. He usually represented it as hybridism, crossbreeding and complete culture as in biology, agriculture, linguistics in order to raise stronger genes. Hence, marriage, despite the fight against one gender, to a great extent still suffered unhealthy and correctible homogeneousness which was grossly too narrow and simplistic. Diverse relationship, diverse culture, diverse encounters, diverse exposure and diverse world were the real thing for Ebube.

Ebube's father was correct in his insight and early prediction. Ebube's early exposure and familiarity with computers paid back dearly. It actually contributed immensely in firing his imagination and conditioning his aspiration and resourcefulness. Even as a student in Canada, he had begun to delve in numerous researches and building some machines and gadgets patent to him. He had emerged early enough one of the many Nigerians making waves positively and wielding influences abroad and across the globe.

Ebube started to speak to the entire house in that morning assembly. Everyone was eager and anticipating his contribution. He provided a better view and approach to help Obi to grow and improve better. Not necessarily keeping away phone or computer from him. Not necessarily giving in to the phobia of the use of gadgets. Not surely in a fast-changing era, the Gadget and Information Age. But ultimately, his opinion and contribution was different and diverse like his very sermon on diverse relationship, diverse exposure, diverse culture, diverse encounters, diverse society, diverse exchange and diverse world. He observed tacitly and cleverly, 'modern world with its attendant digital revolution, no doubt, is here with us and has come to stay.'

HAND, AGE OR BRAIN?

8

Ebube was a big bull of a man. When he was a child and growing up, no one saw it in him. He was so tiny and lanky in his childhood. No one knew he was going to grow into the giant outlook and personality he had become. In Canada, he was not only serious with his studies. He found other things consequential too. He remembered Sophia writing him one day and remarked, 'I shall be dreadfully unhappy to learn that you do nothing else apart from studies.' The message, indeed, sunk and stuck. It was simple but dense and deep. So he acquired that all the aspects of man cohere into one presence else there would be an outbreak of schizophrenia. He got serious with other things as well. No isolation.

Getting a jewelry of a girl like Sophia was not for an inexperienced. He also relaxed well with body building and fitness. Striking a balance was what it was for him; it gave him huge success. He gave himself tremendously to body building and has suddenly transformed to a very formidable, handsome and attractive young man. He was also, like Sophia, the best choice any partner desired to keep for herself.

Ebube's words were as weighty just as his look was. And he was no talkative. He weighed his words and spoke only when necessary. He thanked Obi's father very profoundly and by extension, the entire house for a happy family reunion after many years of staying away and also the amicable resolution on Obi's matter that morning. He had for long been listening so keenly and following the entire proceedings of the meeting reflectively.

Pat replied him:

'You are most welcome Ebube. We know for certain you may have one or two contributions to make in this family matter. Your inputs will be well appreciated. We are waiting, we are anxious and we are listening.'

Ebube spoke up louder:

'The deliberations have been so awesome and immensely productive. I must sincerely applaud everyone, every member of the family for their inputs. All we seek is to see that we do not lose our brother and son to recklessness, rascality and criminality. This is a noble intention and I must again commend it and commend all of our efforts. It is ultimately because of this that I do agree with all the resolutions arrived at. I agree that it is well fitting that we first safeguard the security of Obi which carrying such device about to school and around might endanger him, and also very importantly, to serve him some penalty for his unruly conduct so that the younger ones can learn in deterrence.'

It was clear on the faces of all of them that Ebube had spoken their mind. They loved his remarks. His admission of facts. The high sense of judgment. But Ebube was acting prudent when he asserted and affirmed the entire judgment. Few others like granny who knew him too well waited and looked out for more. They understood he was not yet done. And it came almost immediately.

Ebube did not seem to understand many things. He did not seem to understand why his society would always make age synonymous with education and leadership. And it was why his society did not recognize and make one a professor and a leader until he had gathered much strands of white hair. After a moment of pause, Ebube looked at everyone. He drew all their attention to granny. 'Just take a cursory look at our Mama here. We all grew up with her and we are all conversant with her story.'

Ebube did not have to say more than that to drive his message home. He did not have to bombard and bore his audience with the known long tale. The story of granny was a popular one in the house. Even the grandchildren have listened to it time and again. They recalled and recited it. Just looking at granny alone communicated the message, brought to the memory one of her childhood travails. Granny has become an image and a symbol of preaching and fostering early to school, early education and early exposure to learning. But her story was a total embodiment of the opposite – delayed education, denied education.

Every time granny related her popular story, she indulged in it going way back the lane of childhood history and fixing her mind totally at the old Juona Community Primary school built since the first decade of twentieth century. Granny recalled and recounted with mixed feelings her old experience of wanting to school in that institution. But it took many different failed attempts and years after her first move before she could really start to study there. It was an experience that made granny like most of other of her mates to lag far behind in catching up in school and learning. She eventually did not continue with school and went into marriage.

By the way, at that time, it was very unpopular and uncustomary to see women go to school. It was an enterprise for the male folks. And most times, it was the weak, indolent and the *efulefu* among the men (who lacked maximally the required strength and stamina a 'real man' needed to do hard work in the fields and farms) that were released and collected to school. Even more, granny was not a very good student.

But even more importantly, for reason no one could well explain, granny's hand could not cross through her head to the other side to touch or have contact with the ear very early enough. It took granny about seven different turns and years to finally get admitted into the school. At this time, her hand could barely begin to cross over the head to the other ear. It was also related by her mother that even at that time and age, her hand still did not run through the head to the other side of the ear. Rather, the village headmaster and the school saw the dogged efforts in granny and the family to go to school and eventually gave in to her quest like the biblical parable of Jesus of the fellow that kept knocking relentlessly at the door until a man as wicked and heart hardened as the king finally responded and yielded to the demand.

The truth was that it was very customary many years down the century particularly in the villages to observe strictly the old practice of measuring and determining the appropriate age of going to school and exposure to learning by the sheer crassness of waiting until the child's hand, usually the right hand, could cross through successfully to the other side of the ear while touching the ear. And for reason quite unusual, granny's hand refused to cross or rather it crossed but ultimately failed to grab the other ear successfully and she was denied starting to go to school again and again until she eventually had to satisfy the damn condition at a seventh attempt.

Crossing the hand successfully through the head to the other side of the ear was perhaps the precursor to the modern JAMB hurdle that many did not scale through thereby bearing so negatively on their educational story and academic ambition. It took granny many trials before reaching the goal. But granny was no such child or tender in age. She was grown. She was about ten years for that matter. But granny had a very small stature. And many said it was her small size that equally contributed to her ordeal.

But despite the size, ultimately, it was the hand that determined the starting of school than the size and look one might possess.

Granny felt many times so bad and weak to hear the headmaster always said to her, 'The hand is still not touching the desired ear, though it can cross over the head. We are going to test you again next session. Try again another school opening.'Granny heard 'try again', 'try again' and got tired of hearing it. She was tired of doing again, trying again. She was weary. She was seriously weighed down. Meanwhile, her contemporaries were making it through to school. Particularly, those ones in the city. When they visited the village and interacted with granny, she was confounded and seriously hurt how old she was and yet to start school because of the consideration of her age or hand or whatsoever.

School, western education and formal learning were not so popular then. It was a less desired and rated area of life, ambition and pursuance. So many people were not into it. So many people did not even admire or look in that direction. Other engagements such as going to farm, selling in the markets, working at home and other places were considered far more rewarding and profitable than going to school. But here was granny who admired and wanted it but faced a herculean hurdle of age of school. Coupled with the frustration of long waiting for the right age, attending to other engagements such farms, trade, marriage eventually came in-between and interrupted immensely academic performances. Granny returned with family and parents to the farms and trade at those different times of mission impossible. Even when at long last she made it, all those affairs she had deeply plunged herself into took serious toll on her and did not help very much her productivity academically.

READING CULTURE

9

She walked gracefully standing half a metre over him. He handed over to her some papers he wanted her to help him out submit on Monday in school. It was clearly their first time of meeting. It eventually turned out to become love at first sight. She was just as himself, a student of the prestigious University of Canada. She was bold, beautiful, tall, blonde skin, blue eyes and extremely striking.

That was the first time Ebube saw Sophia on a visit with one of his Nigerian friends. It was few years ago in the past when Ebube was still arriving Canada for the completion of his doctorate degree. He always visited especially during weekends to pass time with Chioma. They always enjoyed the weekend together, sometimes going out or just remaining in the lounge with conversation revolving around life in Nigeria and many old memories about their old school memories in Nigeria and other things. Memories of Nigeria food, music, films etc. They shared. They relished. It was Ebube who started talking about 'the snake girl' and other classics of the early Nollywood entertainment productions as well as the legendary Fela before Chioma eventually started to make tacit contributions. Here feeding on Nigeria food was a luxury. But they made it a duty to use the weekend to always prepare Nigeria dish. Sometimes on Saturday. Other times, it was Sunday. It was memories of Nigeria stories as well. African stories too.

These stories spiced up and made up the chunk of the long time the duo passed long time talking and talking. These stories held their attention for long most part of the time. Sometimes, deep into the night, talking and excited and engrossed in the stories of the rich civilizations of the black race which most times and for a very long have been grossly and inappropriately misrepresented, distorted and denied by the self-absorbed and self-obsessed white man. These stories were long, old, robust and moving. These stories were sometimes stolen, distorted, abandoned and lost to chronic negligence, ignorance, hatred, malice, jealousy, attacks, plagiarism, thievery and denials. For one thing, Chioma and Ebube were never want of discussions and good contents at that. They had them enough about the place of pride of Africa in the development of the global world; about their resourcefulness, originality and ingenious contributions to the advancements of the world. They never searched for what to talk and relish about Africa, about their country, the same way and manner they engaged other stories and accounts of civilizations of other parts of the world. World civilizations. Traditions and encounters.

On the contrary, the problem which usually made the two to stay long in fight was the problem of choice of the numerous great contents about the black race, African civilizations, the beauty of Nigeria to talk about. Moment like this was highly instrumental in helping them internalize and appropriate the old classes they have had in Economics – the singular problem of choice. Making choice in life. Yet, with the two great companions, it was not the choice of what to study, what to eat, what to wear, where to go, what to become in life/future and what have you. It was chiefly where to begin to tell, share and enjoy the great stories of Africa and their noble nation Nigeria. The story of the great Zik or rather Zik of Africa. The story of Awolowo. The story of Tafewa. The story of Joseph Takar. The story Anthony Enahoro. The story of great Macaulay. The tremendous Nile tradition and civilizations.

The Ujamaa ideology. The Ubuntu school. The great and illustrious Shaka the Zulu and the building and founding of the military formation.The brilliant and breathtaking stories of African Resistance against the external incursions, invasions, infiltrations and impositions. The Maji Maji school. The almighty Ogbunikwe with its companion arsenal. The mind-blowing economy and resources of Africa – the oil, gold, copper, diamond, cocoa, cash crops. The Niger Benue conference, the zone and seat of numerous robust civilizations of the sub-Saharan Africa. The tremendous art renaissance and artistic development with the illustrious Nok culture that eventually birthed latter artistic traditions of west Africa, Bura of Niger (3rd century CE – 10th century CE), Koma of Ghana (7th century CE – 15th century CE), Igbo-Ukwu of Nigeria (9th century CE – 10th century CE), Jenne-Jeno of Mali (11th century CE – 12th century CE), and Ile Ife of Nigeria (11th century CE – 15th century CE). The stories of the ultimate struggles, movements and fights for independence, from total liberation from the shackles of the colonialists and conquistadors. Indeed, the long walk to freedom. But they did not always celebrate the paper kind of freedom of their country and by extension, the entirety of the continent of Africa.

Despite the fact that the two erudite Africans measured majorly in the sciences, they made extreme efforts not to forget the first canon of all learned men and the first mark of scholarship – versatility, diversity, universality - the ability to know little of everything. They read. They read. And they read well. They had been doing so since they were much younger. They both enjoyed early exposure at childhood. They were passionately exposed to literatures, history and their own history at that. It was Chioma who always quoted Professor Wole Soyinka, 'books and all forms of writings are terror to those oppose the truth'. They knew enough that history and literatures are the first foundation and principle. They understood that there was no science or scientific revolutions which were anything more than periods of historical upheavals when existing traditions and scientific ideas were replaced by new paradigms. Beyond just telling and sharing and relishing these stories, Ebube had started putting his writing arts together. He wrote most times during his leisure in the bid to recreate many lost and rich legacies of Africa. He was certain that one of the biggest problems that is negatively affecting African studies, African knowledge, African civilization and all Africans is the problem of writing and proper documentations.

Chioma was a medical student, very intelligent and pretty. Just like Ebube and Chioma, there were equally numerous other Nigerians and Africans studying and thriving very well in the institution and in Canada with other endeavors and commitments. Today, it was not the company of two as usual. There was definitely a third party. They were three. Sophia had joined the company belatedly in the evening to visit with Chioma her friend.

But beyond her body and appearance, Sophia was curious and such a searching mind, desirous and ready to learn; always prepared and disposed to update and upgrade herself. Let say she was just like her friend (s) in the house. Hence a perfect demonstration of the old aphorism, 'birds of a feather fly together' or 'show me your friend and I will tell you who you are'. This was particularly what endeared Sophia to Ebube. A good friend of his friend, his early impression about her was demonstrative of the level of inquisitiveness and intelligence she possessed. He asked Chioma after one of the books he kept with her and he was told that Sophia collected the book for reading. He was impressed about her admiration for exposure to books.

Just before she parted for the kitchen where she was partly helping her friend out to make Nigeria food, he asked,

'Are you still with my book?'

'Yes.'

'Are you done studying the book?'

'No', she answered quite promptly and proceeded quite innocently to disclose (to him) her biggest obstacle in her candid inquiry,

'Someone discouraged me from continuing with the book, is it true that l should stop?'

'And who is the person?'

'My roommate.'

'And who is your lodge mate?'

'You may not know her even if l told you…'

'Or is she Chioma? Don't be scared of her presence, tell me the truth? I know her too well. She is not a good reader.'

'No, she is not. She is not my lodge mate.'

'Okay, so, whosoever this person could be, why did she ask you to discontinue reading the book?''

'She said that the book is evil, devilish, demonic…''

The name of the book is *DIGITAL FORTRESS* by Don Brown. It is a book loaded with the stories and operations of powerful machines and programs. The smartest of the machines which was a program running with no stop was the digital fortress on which the entire narrative revolved around. Ebube was sure of one thing. He was certain that it was the customary obsessive fears that had affected Sophia too and prevented her from finding out what the book was automatically all about.

Ebube was quiet for some time. He was not sure of what to say or how to begin to speak to her. He took a deep breath while struggling on the right way and manner to speak to her glaring innocence. First, he said to her 'let's pretend that what your friend said about the book is a gospel truth, at least let's allow ourselves to be fooled easily for a while.' Then, he proceeded thus:

'Way back in Nigeria in my high school,the guy who was quite renowned in his exorcism ministry read and watched things on demons always. Understudying and always watching demons did not make him a demon or a devil but on a contrary, a destroyer of demons. But before he could do so, he ought to have a robust knowledge and understanding of the demons. He was called a very powerful and spiritual Catholic priest.'

'Stop confusing the little girl', Chioma jerked from the pantry.

'Again, there was a great man and scholar known in history as Karl Marx of German descent, a rare genius, highly perspicacious and forceful in intellectualism.'

'Yes, I know him, I have read him ....'

'Good to know...He was a man who it is very easy to mistake for a capitalist given his numerous studies, writings and understanding on capitalism. In fact, his second book after the popular *Communist Manifestoes* in 1848 at the end of the Second World War was called *the Capital* published in 1867. But on the contrary, Karl Marx was a thorough-going socialist, a socialist revolutionary and the father of socialism whose energy and influence did so much to produce numerous staunch socialists across the world to initiate and ignite socialist movements and revolutions in Europe, Africa, Asia et al. Walter Rodney, Frantz Fanon, Almicar Cabral, Julius Nyeyere, Kwame Nkrumah, Zik of Africa, Leopold Senghor and many others. The list is long. But Marx's critical understudy of capitalism was only a way to understand and destroy it.'

Sophia smiled. She was gaining interest and was keenly enthralled in the lecture. She momentarily recalled a few facts she knew about these personalities. Practically any good student could tell at the tip of hand the great thoughts and feats these tremendous human agencies engendered, embodied and committed to the world of their time and beyond. Walter Anthony Rodney Walter was a Guyanese historian, political activist and academic who embedded in his masterpiece, *How Europe Underdeveloped Africa* so much Marxist ideas and liberation struggles. He was assassinated in 1980. Franz Omar Fanon Frantz, born in 1925 and died in 1965, was a French West Indian psychiatrist and political philosopher from the French colony of Martinique, and he immortalized his being and powerful ideas in his *Wretched of the Earth* and other writings. His works have become influential in the fields of post-colonial studies, critical theory and Marxism. Almicar Lopez da Costa Cabral, born in 1924 and died in 1973 was a man of many parts: a Bissau-Guinean and Cape Verdean agricultural engineer, pan-Africanist, intellectual, poet, theoretician, revolutionary, political organizer, nationalist and diplomat. He was one of Africa's foremost anti-colonial leaders who held that government is institutionalized violence and only counter violence can undo it. Julius

Kambarage Nyereye was a Tanzanian anti-colonial activist, politician, and political theorist who founded the ujamaa theory. Léopold Sédar Senghor was a Senegalese poet, politician and cultural theorist, first president of Senegal, ideologically an African socialist, and the major theoretician of Négritude. Kwameh Nkrumah was a founding father of Ghana, the first president in Africa and the founder and father of consciencism. While Nnamdi Benjamin Azikiwe who enshrined his own ideas in zikism was, like Awolowo and Tafewa Balewa, a founding father of modern Nigeria or the giant of Africa. Ebube completed,

'Instances abound and inexhaustible. There are people whose field of study is criminology, or a branch of law called criminal law. Understudying any of these is not to make a criminal of them but to rather fight and curb criminality. Tell me the truth, let's pretend the book is actually bad, how do you deal with evil without first knowing it?'

Ebube was done in quick minutes. It was now Sophia's own turn to take a deep breath. She thanked him profusely. She left in silence but very much illuminated and relieved. Chioma made more joke of Ebube asking him not to teach nonsense to her friend. They were all amused. They got to other discussions surrounding studies, school, sports and the previous Friday club. It was superb, they all confessed and shared intimately. It was there that Ebube should have first seen Sophia but he was deeply overwhelmed with other colleagues and chats. When Sophia was done with her visit and wanted to go home, Ebube saw her off. Inwardly, Chioma had started putting one and two together in the head. The amusing Chioma even teased them again and again of falling in love in her place. On the way, the two talked deeper and more intimately. Sophia continued to show appreciation to Ebube for his insight at the house. They revisited the conversation. Sophia was the first to start. What she said appeared like the proceed of the long lecture she had just received.

'What has gone wrong over time in our society is that most people especially in the misguided theme of religion or rather ridiculous piety, have consciously and consistently given themselves up to petty and shallow exposure, living without expecting and getting so much from life. People do not want to open up their mind, stretch themselves, widen their horizons, participate in the fast changing digital space and become bigger than they know, than they are. There is indeed alarming level of the syndrome and pathology of self-preoccupation, self-absorption.'

'Yes, I agree with you. It is so bad that seeking knowledge and exploring and daring the unknown has been hastily labeled evil and demonic. This is a generation where observations, questions, experimentations, researches and critical studies are speedily dying out because our shallow and blind religiosity betrays us to call them evil, to stigmatize and demonize them.'

Seriously, Ebube never expected all that to be coming from Sophia. He was amazed at her contributions. Whatsoever he had for her inside him was given more flame. He was made to say more:

'Timid and shallow people will easily misinterpret and misrepresent so many things they do not only understand but more ultimately they do not even desire to demonstrate the least readiness and disposition to understand at all for obvious reason – they label it evil, ungodly. Timid and shallow children of God know very little about the science of fight, sex, alcohol, drugs, contraceptives, rape, cultism, politics, power, fashion, music, criminality, prostitutions, romance, self-defense, war, revolts, arms, weaponry, intrigues, secrecy, conspiracy, lies, tactics, strategies, etc. They jettison and ignore all these and treat them as inconsequential. But ironically, they ought to live with all these in the world whether they like it or not.'

'They even know very little or practically nothing about body fitness, economy, government, computer, sciences, cosmology, histories or other literatures outside their faith, doctrines and beliefs. Timid and shallow lives.'

'They would easily get lost in any relevant discussion that revolves around any of these. For them entertainment world and show business is of no consequence. For whose sake? Who cares? Timid and shallow minds have practically nothing to say or contribute in a political and socio-economic discourse. They easily but erroneously abscond from the society understanding practically nothing on how the economy works, how government operates. They know nothing about government policies and growing the economy. Even election is treated with utmost disdain and negligence. What happens at the polls, not the pulpit, does not matter at all to them. Who loses or wins in elections is not of their concern. They may not even tell the names of their political leaders and representatives. It is for whose sake?'

In no short time, it appeared as if Sophia was leading the discussion. She said with boldness:

'Timid and shallow minds would not engage in any conversations that revolve around sex and romance. Or read or study a thing on them. They are shy and scared to know about (their) sexuality. For them, sex education is for whose sake? Who cares? Since, it has to do with sex, it is automatically and conclusively immoral, bad, evil, unholy, ungodly, unspeakable, forbidden, a taboo, an abomination and therefore no-go-area (mercury) but efforts have begun on going to the mercury. So, case closed. Except you choose deliberately and stubbornly to be mad, immodest, deviant, weird, outlaw, unholy, ungodly, evil, devilish, demonic, satanic, etc like some of us. But unfortunately, after all said and done, they cannot help but face the reality every day because no one can afford to lie to him or herself or chide away from the reality (even when you do, inside you, you know the truth). Reality is reality.'

'Timid and shallow minds limit and restrict themselves only to their own area of study, learning, profession or field of expertise without searching into others to understand (of course, not everything or even so much) but at least a thing, a little about other endeavours and fields which would make them diverse, versatile, broad and connecting. I could be a devout and holy pastor but that is not a yardstick for me not to know something about trade or how my car or generator operates. A student or scholar in sciences can still be knowledgeable in management studies, politics, philosophy, history or other fields of life.'

Their talk went for long. They did not plan it. Chioma did not know they were going to stay so long in their walk. They themselves did not know so. But they enjoyed their time together. The discussion had flowed beyond expectation. It had flowed effortlessly. They allowed nature to take its course. They relished the moment. They talked about lunch. Ebube asked and Sophia was willing. 1:30 in the afternoon, they two consented mutually. It marked the beginning of the lovely relationship between Ebube and Sophia. Almost in an amusing way as Sophia was taking bus, one remark came from each of the lovers to reiterate their conversation today. Ebube was the first:

'What we do not recommend is a society or holy people who would understand very little or nothing of the things in the world, their own immediate surroundings. And as if that is not enough, they celebrate it as mark of piety. We do not recommend a pious people who cannot negotiate business or who do not understand at least the basic intrigues in politics, economy etc. We do not want to grow or breed a people who are fools in matters of sex, who do not follow the trend of issues, who know very little or nothing about medical science, security, wars, arms, weaponry, computer, engineering sciences, the science of agriculture and production; religious who are clueless about cosmology, astronomy and other matters and subjects of immense and fundamental importance. We do not want pious people who are bereft of ideas.'

'And of course, and conversely, what we do not recommend in any sense is a people, citizens and nations that are clueless, detached and inexperienced of the things and ways of God, holiness and total spirituality. For the latter would even be more implicative, and of more adverse consequence than the former. And so with even greater vigour, energy, vehemence and insistence, we want to emphasize, enforce and push for the latter.'

'See you tomorrow', said ….?

'Catch you too', … responded enthusiastically.

THE RESOLUTION

10

One of those who have assisted and contributed, many said, to the long deliberation and fruitful resolution of the family was not truly a member of the family. Was it not said that man's help could emanate from anywhere especially outside his own very home, outside his own kinsmen and kindred? And again: if a prophet is not regarded in his own place, then he would be regarded in another place. The name of the outsider and unknown prophet was veronica. She was the diverse figure among the homogenous home. She was the necessary unlike-term in the mathematical equation. She created truly a diverse membership in the long discussion. She was regarded in another place and home unlike her own home. She had not been part of the family assembly since the morning conference. She had been in the visitor's room overhearing part of the conversation at some points or intervals.

Some said she was a visitor that followed Ebube on his journey back home. Others said she was just one of the visitors that warmed up Mr Pat's house, for the good man (Pat) loved helping and receiving visitors or strangers like the Judaic Abraham of old. This same group of people also judged so early that, just like Abraham, Pat did not know when he had received an angel that would eventually transform the conversation and bring immense contribution and resolution in the family matter. Yet, there were those that said that she was a neighbor who found refuge and security in the home of Pat the previous night after the beating and domestic violence her husband caused and unleashed on her. What shocked a lot of people was her gross silence and inaction in the terrible situations she was subjected to or she subjected herself rather. People's worries were two folds: why on earth would human beings and men in this case, in this Age and time still engage in the barbaric, uncultured and animalistic lifestyle of beating their wives and subjecting them to pains and hell?

The second was if she actually wanted to die before she could do the needful, before she could do something about her life? Worse still, she would not allow others to intervene between her and her 'beloved husband'. She has in that manner stopped Mr Pat at different many occasions from confronting the man and to make him face the law accordingly. Some said she was bewitched by the man. Others said that no spell was as dangerous and deadly as the spell of religious shackles, religious sham and religious shame that have over time and across different situations in history stopped many people from truly living, from the true authentic life of freedom, choice and responsibility. The irrationality which most religious people are predisposed and guided has not helped her to temper faith with common sense or reason. Regardless of those speculations, what was certain and important to the family at the moment was the uninvited way and manner and the courage with which Mrs Veronica entered into discussion with promising and positive effects.

'Children of these days? Forget them, they can fool you into the well, cover you up and not even blink', Mrs Veronica walking close to the family assembly from a glassy staircase coffered out. The glassy staircase was the only expensive acquisition Mr Pat had spent so much money regardless of his usual frugal lifestyle. It reflected the image of the users as clear as the most powerful camera in the world. Some said that the staircase also doubled as a lifter for those who could not really take a long walk up and down the building. It possessed electronic building like some other parts of the building.

'Madam, good morning. I am sorry, this is a family talk. Pick your breakfast from the refectory and return to your room', Obi's mother reacted. But granny was of a different point of view. Some of the family members stood with Obi's mother and others supported granny. They dragged it among themselves for a moment.

'I insist, this is purely family matter. No one gives the food meant for the children to the dog', Obi's mother strengthened her argument

'You have spoken well, my daughter. But many are coming from the east and west and taking their place even before the sons and daughters of the kingdom. We have come to a point that we must understand that diverse interaction, interchange and exchange of discussion and ideas places us in the position to understand problems and situations of life better', granny fought back even more persuasively.

'My beloved people, in my humble submission, I still think that this matter is not yet beyond us and there should be no public in our midst'

'My daughter, what you are yet to learn is that no one can see the edifice only from inside. Outside view is very important. Diversity will make a big difference, diversity is God's gift of innovation. Things of value are things that are different not necessarily alike. Let her say something before leaving us', granny submitted.

'We must make stringent efforts to fight and resist and conquer the fear of accepting those who are not like us', Ebube added. He had been looking like a deaf and dumb fellow since the commencement of the brief polemic between granny and Obi's mother. He had been sitting on the fence refusing to take side. But everyone knew for sure where Obi's vote was meant for. His remark did not, therefore, take anyone by surprise. It was much expected just as the speaker intended it. In the end, the party of granny seemed to have won without rigging or malpractice. Mrs Veronica finally spoke and made her contribution.

'Children of these days', Mrs Veronica continued, 'these children will not kill us'

Everyone gave a resounding 'amen' again and again.

'This is exactly what my own daughter did to me too some years ago'

Mrs Veronica finally plunged into the full story of one of the shocking events in her life. Few years ago, her daughter made her to see the danger of modern day technology, phone and internet. The girl was not actually her daughter but she has taken her to be one especially as an African mother. The true mother of the girl had died so painfully but more neglectfully and recklessly during childbirth. The complication of the birthing process was quite surmountable and avoidable if not for the dearth of medical facilities and unequipped health institutions in the country by long years of wicked and poor leadership.

After the death of the mother, veronica raised up the girl child. Today, the girl called her mother. No one could possibly tell that she was not the biological mother. Lucy was the name of the girl. She was just fifteen years old when the painful incidence occurred.

Lucy was sent to one of the model colleges in Abuja. It was a boarding school. The school did not even allow phones or any of the modern gadgets for the use of the students. The school was really strict and stern in the old tradition than the numerous indulgences registered in most schools today. It gave her (foster) mother a quick impression that she would be well disciplined and focused on her studies without allowing distractions in her life. She was already in SSS2 class.

It was resumption day for Lucy. She had resumed in her school uniform because the school always insisted that the students must dress properly. That day, the mother went to drop Lucy in school. She was in her green check house wear. Lucy went to the dormitory with her brother who helped her to settle in, carrying her luggage. While the mother was at the bursar's office settling the outstanding fees and showing receipts for other payments she had made for books. She was engaged in some financial sorting.

Her younger daughter came back to meet her on the queue at the bursar's office and told her that Lucy was settled. Lucy and the girl called each other sisters even though they were not. By the time she was done at the bursar's office, because there were lots of parents and guardians too who came to settle financial issues with the bursar, it was too late. So she told the daughter to go to tell her sister she would come to visit before month's end. The mother also could not see Lucy before leaving because it was already time when the bell goes for students to go into their hostels for head count. The school always did head count every evening especially upon resumption. Many of the students loitering around the premises ran into the hostels to be counted. Then the mother and her son departed. She was happy and confident that she had done her job as a mother.

Three days later, however, she was called by her daughter's house mistress asking for Lucy. Her impulsive reaction was expected.

'Huh, what are you talking about?'

'Your daughter has not resumed school and I am wondering what has happened to her'

'Haba! Are you dreaming? I brought her to school on Sunday, she resumed with the rest of her mates on the resumption day'

The house mistress stayed on what she said explaining that for three days no one has seen Lucy, yet her bed was always made. Lucy' mother practically ran mad that day. She raced to the school like an escapee from an asylum. She was in a turmoil. She was weak and drained. She went practically white and froze. Her kneels knocked. She remembered very well that she drove her daughter to school herself, and she was checked into the hostel by the house mistresses' assistant. Where on earth could she be then?

She got to school to see things for herself. Lo and behold, it was all true. It was not a dream or a joke or something of sort. The house mistress summoned Lucy's close friend to the office. The mistress wanted to find out who had been laying her bed and fooling them for the past days she had been absent from school premises. A laid bed supposes that the owner of the space was around. The friends had been laying her bed, making the hostel staff to believe she was around. Empty beds or unlaid beds meant otherwise, the student had not returned to school. The house mistress invited three of Lucy's friends and interrogated them for a while. But they did not speak up. They did not tell her the truth until after serious minutes of tortures. It was at this point that they began to confess one after the other like thieves and witches. The girls were brought to the principal's office to severe the engagement.

The girls cried and cried. They confessed that Lucy had met one boy on Facebook who invited her to come to visit him at one hotel. Unfortunately, Lucy's friends did not know the name of the hotel. But they were the ones that provided a detailed information of how it happened. When the mother had dropped her in school wearing her house wear, she had gone into the hostel and changed to mufti. Lucy's mother did not know that Lucy smuggled mufti into her bag even when the mother had insisted that she was going to pack the bag herself and she did. The mother gazed for long standing like a tree that has been abandoned for long without ritual offerings and rites. She did not know when she coughed out, 'the more you look, the less you see'. 'I agree absolutely with you mummy Obi when you said that your mother told you that one can feed the stomach as well as s/he wishes but it will still find something for itself without one knowing it. After all the efforts she put in to ensure something discrediting was not taken to the school, Lucy still had her way.

Mrs Veronica knew now that all she fought and wanted to avoid has eventually become her guest. She deliberately chose to pack the bag herself because she suspected she would go to school with contraband. But even at that, she remembered that the school checked students' boxes upon resumption. She could not really tell or imagine how she managed to do what she did. Indeed, Mrs Veronica meant it when she said that 'these children can fool you'.

Hence, the search for Lucy began in earnest. The search began from the hostels. Every look and cranny were combed. The entire school premises were under surveillance. She was nowhere to be found. No one saw her. The search continued with her photos displayed asking for her whereabouts. Different police stations were visited and reports were successfully made. For two days, there was no news of Lucy. For two days, the mother and the family mourned and worried. The mother did not sleep. She did not equally eat anything because she believed in her heart that someone has deceived her child.

It was afterthought for her to realize that her child was not the little innocent she thought she was after all. Lucy had been chatting with the guy and she agreed to come and visit him. She had changed to mufti in the evening and walked herself out of the school premises disguised as a cleaner for what she wanted to do. Worse still, the mother did not know that she had a phone. She did not buy a phone for her because she could not afford it. So she gave Lucy an old phone she had used before but Lucy complained that the phone could not do internet and so she dropped it. It made the mother to think that Lucy had no phone with her all the while. She did not have the idea that Lucy had another phone. But in all this, Lucy's whereabouts mattered to her more than all else, more than any judgment or analysis at the moment.

It was the last day of the week of the search that Lucy was seen dumped early in the morning around 5:00am at the school gate. Lucy was raped again and again by her predators. It was a painful sight. It was graphic. She had red blotches all over her body. She suffered several lacerations on her vagina. She had broken rib. Her face was badly swollen and red with blood. Her hands and feet had been tied during the acts. Lucy experienced hell on earth. Walking and urinating was so terrible and a painful sight to behold. She was barely alive when they dumped her at the school gate. Maybe, they had the news of the search for Lucy particularly the involvement of the cops, and were afraid of being caught. But nobody was sure of anything.

It was few days later at the sickbed in the hospital that Lucy related her experience to her mother with tears and begging, promising to turn a new leaf. Lucy was to many people a good girl. The mother could swear with her life that she was well behaved and disciplined. She was quiet. She did not go out even on holidays. Many occasions, the mother almost went on her kneel before Lucy could accept to go and make deliveries for her. She preferred being indoors, watching TV etc. but here Lucy was lying down in the hospital for three weeks helplessly just all because of cell phone technology and internet space. Mrs Veronica's pain seemed to reinvigorate at the retelling of the story. But it was not pain or anger or any emotion from Lucy or the school or anyone at all. It was pain and anger that have ultimately transformed to passionate phobia built around cell phone technology and internet especially in the lives of the youths. She supported Obi's father for going to put away the use of internet by Obi.

Lucy passed three weeks in the hospital. She also got suspension from the school for her punishment as a deterrent for others to learn. The story had gone out that she was setting a bad example in the school. She nearly did not want to return to school after the suspension. But the mother insisted and made her to complete her education. She was ashamed and did not want to go back to the school. She repeated class but it was just one year behind her mates. The mother granted her her request of going to a different school which gave her the neutral ambiance to learn and improve. But ultimately, the good news today is what has become of Lucy. She truly regretted her action. She truly repented. Sometimes, experience truly is the best teacher. The mother and the entire family and the society at large were so proud of her. Today, Lucy mentors younger girls and advises them against the dangers of internet.

Listening to Mrs Veronica and her long tale, the entire members of the house were froze momentarily. They all sat practically lame, deaf and dumb and starring directionless like those who power had gone out of. Somewhat Mrs Veronica has not helped in the direction of the already existing fear surrounding cell phone technology and internet space. Her story has rather helped to build up more fear and rejection and interdiction of the use of cell phones. But the story has also helped them to understand more the experience of the youths especially adolescents and the use of cell phones and the possible negative impacts and implications that even destroy many.

The handwriting was clearly written following the catalyst story all the family members had just listened to, fueling their minds and increasing the palpitation. There would be no leniency at all and no compromise in keeping Obi away from the use of cell phone regardless of the amount of argument and quality of eloquence with which Ebube must develop and deliver his lecture, campaign, advocacy and novelty on adventures, exposure to modern technology, intelligence and learning.

11

When Ebube invited everybody to look at granny, he was definitely and invariably passing across a deep message. He was committed ultimately in preaching and fostering early education and early exposure to learning and technology as different and opposed to delayed and consequently denied education. But the presence of Mrs Veronica has no doubt introduced diversity and complexity in his achieving this. He was seen looking like one struggling with regret, regretting why he supported the intervention and contribution of the visitor. But that was only a momentary thought or emotion. He improved his imagination and thought. He realized soon that for his argument or position to be good enough and sustainable, it has to witness diverse and complex opposition, a thought or position different from his. He needed an argument that differed extensively from his in order to engender a superior thought. He recalled quickly how he had said that people must make stringent efforts to fight and resist and conquer the fear of accepting those who are not like them. Ebube could not take back his words. Mrs Veronica, surely offered him that opportunity and platform of diversity.

Bigger than that was the demonstration of his ingenious mind to draw strength from Veronica's story. Ebube pointed out strongly that while discipline and training of the young ones are not negotiable and cannot be compromised, fear, taboo and rejection of technology, exposure and learning cannot be an option either. There must be a middle ground. Not to spoil the child with phone technology and internet space and very importantly, not to make them daft and dumbs about the brilliant Age of internet space, technological gadgets, scientific revolution, information, communication, intelligence and learning. The young ones needed to be aware and awake to them now not in their old age or belatedly as it was the story of granny and many others. 'Technology should make us aware not weary', Ebube remarked. Ebube had a few moment of exchangeand cross examination with Mrs Veronica before she parted.

'Your story deeply touched and moved all of us and it still does and would not be forgotten in a haste', Ebube stopped momentarily while everyone gave a quiet nod in affirmation before he continued.

'We are glad that Lucy is a better person today. It is what matters most. The experience was part of the processes of growing up, of adventure though reckless adventure at that which all of us had in our own different ways and times. I want you to regard this good news aspect of it more than anything else, more than the pains and losses. I said this more because it appears that you are yet with phobia and anger and closed mind concerning phone technology particularly for the young ones and you don't seem to notice the side of positivity'

'Yes, I do. What is bad is bad'

'Yes, I agree. But we have first to figure out the bad aspect. It is not wise to cut off the leg or toes because of the grown nails'

'But if cutting off the toes is necessary, if it is what will save life, why not yes? I support it absolutely. Even the Holy Book said something of sort. I am not the author: If the eyes or leg would cause one to go to the hellfire, they are better removed for it is better to stay without legs or eyes in heaven than to stay and suffer in hellfire with them. In this same way, I choose to say that it is more fitting to stay without phone gadgets than to suffer the corruption and ignoble damageof having and keeping them, the damned pains and losses that come with them'

'Wow, in that case, the use of cell phone technology and internet space should be totally cut off from the young ones?'

'Yes of course. This technology adventure is causing us to lose our children steadily and repeatedly'

'Well, it will interest you to know that the cause is not phone technology adventures but reckless adventure at that. There is a big demarcation between the two. But people do not oftentimes know it, they do not pay attention to the difference. Driving does not cause accidents or death but reckless driving and ignorance. And so it is with other things of life too'

'Well said. I support you in this', Mrs Veronica managed to say.

 'May I find out something from you?'

'And what is that?'

Would you rather have to choose that there is no flying adventures for people or for Daedalus and his son just because of fears of destruction or to choose flying adventures that will bring people out from the dungeon of caves and captivity; bondage and backwardness?'

She was mute for the passing seconds until she said, 'this is a difficult decision. But bondage and backwardness are not good'

'Well, I am happy to say to you that no one can fly without technology, without phone gadgets in our own time and space'

'So in that case, we can only manage it, deal with it, manage technology not abrogation or total cut off? So you mean?'

'Remember Lucy had many things cut off from her'

'How do you mean please?'

'You never bought phone for Lucy and she did not want to use the single purpose phone you gave her. The school too did not permit the use of phone also. Do these measures and others not look like the cut off strategy and panacea you campaign for?'

Mrs Veronica was mute and bemused momentarily and finally managed to cough out, 'yes, it is. I think they are'

'Remember also how thorough you searched her bag and you insisted on packing it yourself. Remember still that Lucy from record was not outgoing even during holidays she stayed indoors. Don't all these add up to the cut off remedy including self-inflicted ones?'

'I have answered before. But why these questions, why asking me…?' Mrs Veronica said almost with pain'

'It is simple, my dear sister and friend. It is pointing to us as a people, as parents and guardians and as a moral society that total cut off, taboos, prohibitions, fears, disconnects and denying our children things such as these or adventures do not help them to grow better. It kills and destroys them more in secret and pretense. It only has to be managed for technology is here with us. We cannot ignore that fact. It is not to spoil them with it and it is also not to spoil them without it. A middle ground must always be found'

Mrs Veronica was quiet.

'I have said this before and I will continue to say it. Technology including cell phone and internet space should help us to be aware not weary' Ebube added. When Mrs Veronica had exhausted her time and retired to her room, Ebube continued to address the house.

'History is very powerful and not many people learn from it. History can keep repeating itself not necessarily in the same very way it occurred before but assuming different forms. Or rather, speaking in a more technical manner: history does not repeat itself but a continuation, a continuum. I am quick to notice here in our very midst the continuation of the old tradition, which granny and many others were victims of, but in a different form; I notice here in our very midst an acute tendency to delay and withhold education, exposure; I notice here a deep silent hesitation and repulsion to school. Not the traditional or regular school that we know very much about but the school of exposure, the school of technology, gadgets. The question I have for all of us is: are we going to keep Obi waiting like it was done to granny or would we rise to the occasion and braze up with courage not phobia to the new society that has richly evolved in order to break away from the old habit?'

Obviously, Ebube was strongly opposed to total cut off and taboos on modern technology, something that vexed and irritated him badly. Maybe, because he was a big time beneficiary of early childhood exposure. He pointed out how youths and children play around and manipulate technological gadgets and even build them in other parts of the world. But his own people and society continued to make technology strange and strangers to their own children and world. He pointed out that the old tradition that stayed many children from gaining entrance into school has only took change of hands and it was yet to be over. Presently, in his own time and society, there might not be the crass practice of waiting until the right hand runs through the head to the other ear but there was in the system and mind the subsistence of the old mentality still thriving in keeping the young ones from early participation and early exposure grounded chiefly on age rather than ability and purpose and reason. He suffered it still at the university before leaving the country where he was blatantly denied what he merited and deserved just because of his young age. For him, it was clearly no more a rule written down in book but still systemic and largely in the mindset. Ebube added rather suddenly.

'Sixteen and getting to seventeen, Obi cannot be stopped from interaction and familiarity with modern computers and machines for no justified cause other than fear and protecting him and waiting for university or rather age, just like our granny here. It is why he is beginning to own it and indulge in it so secretly.'

Ebube, therefore, proceeded to fault some aspect of the deliberations that excused and relieved Obi maximally from the use of smart phone or computer until higher institution just as it was the ultimate rule in most homes and institutions most times grounded on fears, and empty fears at that. He pointed out boldly that what he did not pray for was to build a culture where any people or the family would propagate and promote learning only and mostly at old age and it was common among many people of the less civilized and pre-scientific society. This crass tradition has caused several adults not to know and maneuver the use of gadgets, computers. In fact, it has succeeded in breeding a certain level of phobia in the use of machines or technology. That most people expressed acute hesitation and reservation in the use of machines including university graduates, educated adults, teachers in the schools, parents at homes and leaders in the government. He pointed out that time and the world were speedily changing and all people owed it as a sacred duty to change alongside and conform. It was a machine and gadget Age and Obi must participate in it; particularly as he was a student needing certain findings and learning online even as a college student. Ebube did not stop reminding all members of the family that it is the task of all people to be aware and not weary of modern technology and its transformation and impacts. Computer was a basic tool and it was speedily becoming a common household facility. Though the family might block Obi access to it but the worse danger was that he would indulge willfully in secrecy and do in secret what they blatantly denied and refused him openly.

Everyone was able to understand that the usual religious and moral temperament of the family as well as fear of modern technology has contributed immensely to the decision and lifestyle of protecting Obi from using smart phone at his age or until he got to the university. But it shocked them to learn from Ebube sharing his critical and profound understanding that gadgets are school, technology is a school, phone is a school,and computeris a school. They are the new school. He was quick to liken it to the arrival of the first and traditional school and the repulsive and unwelcoming attitude towards it. The fear many people harboured that kept them away from releasing their children to school for school was viewed almost like corrupting them, sacrificing them, giving them to nuisance, wastefulness and unrewarding ventures. It was why only the *efulefu* were sent or permitted to go to school. The weak, lazy and unproductive ones.Today, Ebube cautioned that this should not be the case with the new school of gadgets, of technology, of phones, of computers that so many still thought with shocking phobia that exposure to digital life was a wasteful venture and only destructive to the users. Some even thought it was satanic and demonic and kept their distance.

Ebube was still talking when a message came into his cell phone. The message was coming from his elder sister. She was reminding him about visiting with her before leaving the country. Her name was Dorcas. For one thing, it was difficult for Ebube to comprehend the happenstance. Just at the time he was addressing the phobia and different ways modern technology was demonized, his sister was communicating him.

Dorcas, Ebube's elder sister, did not have the will and ambition to studying long Ebube. Not even like any other member of the family. She managed to come through with her primary school. Coupled with little knowledge and her alarming religious temperament, she rejected using phone technology labeling it as satanic. But after many years, she came to admit the fact that she should no longer live outside the reality. Gradually, she adjusted and loosened her doctrinal teachings, taboos and restrictions.

Ebube strongly held that Obi could not be completely dispensed from using smart phone. That would amount invariably to dropping out of school. The name of the school was modern gadgets. And age should be no barrier to the school. Obi could not be made to drop out of that school to suffer culture lag in matters of gadget and technology. Not certainly by the way of avoidance and total detachment which Ebube judged as throwing away both the bowel with the baby.

Ebube went to the bed that night seriously enthralled and entangled in his lone thought concerning the entire development during the day. He understood particularly from his own early experience that people must not have to wait until late hour, older age to be exposed to good life or better life, to knowledge and exploration if they could have it done earlier but prescribing safety. Obi was grown enough and must have to begin to be exposed to gadgets and computers not until he had got to the university.This gave Ebube intense worry and kept him thinking through the night. His main point was to show strong disagreement for anything whatsoever that was the foundation for judging Obi too young to use smart android phone in the Age of information and communication at that, until he had gone into the university. 'Why does African society stay back the growth, maturity, exposure and productivity of her children?' Ebube did not know when that question came out of his mouth while he was still thinking through the whole event. At university level, Obi should not just be starting to learn to use such gadgets but should be preoccupied with something else more advanced. He should not be battling yet with such elementary knowledge of gadgets and their uses, applications and technicalities: how to follow classes online; send email and other correspondences; manage accounts, adds, applications and more but something far more sophisticated. Obi lived in a larger world and had his contemporaries to compete with favorably and globally. Obi must not have to begin to learn the science of machines and master computer only at such later or advanced age particularly where the means and safety to do so can be provided. 'What I advocate is that a more modest smart phone, not necessarily the pompous and ostentatious iPhone, should be provided both for his own use and learning, or I should say exposure', Ebube had finally submitted before the family dismissal.

His judgment in Obi's matter was not easily welcomed. It took some passing days of consideration and reconsideration. Some supported him. Others did not and were the party who were on the side of waiting till Obi was an adult before he could be allowed to access what seemed to them too risky for his age. Ebube also went ahead to make a case so that Obi's parents acquire, not just for Obi but for the younger siblings (Anita, Ngozi and Cheta), smart phones for all to learn technology and be part of the fast-changing digital sphere. Let say thatEbube also gained victory at a second judgment. This concerned the choice of place of university study for Obi when soon he got finally done with his college. The father had also in the course of long deliberations, because of the questionable character of Obi, ruled and insisted vehemently thatObi was not moving away from home for his university education. His university education must be in the same place he had practically lived all his life in order for him to stay close to home for a closer surveillance.

At a face value, this was also another seeming very plausible judgment the house had reached and ruled for the betterment of the loose and recalcitrant boy. Yet, for Ebube, the house could do better than the judgment they had come up with from the long period of family conclave. His position at this second deliberation was simply that it would still amount to the same serious disfavor and disadvantage and disservice to the boy, just as the first, to have him run his university study in the same place he was born, passed his childhood, had his primary school and secondary school. Phobia or chronic fear and parochialism was the principal cause for such a judgment which many would readily jump at basking in the euphoria of elation for going to stay away from the new or strange cultures of other places and peoples. Ebube saw through it. He was fully aware and abreast with such common developments resulting from provincialism and shallow mindedness and circumscribed culture. He told the house a proverb that says, 'a man's feet should be planted at home but his eyes should go round and traverse the universe'. How was it possible for Obi's eyes (and the most important of eyes is the mind or mind eyes) to traverse the globe following such a drastic and circumscribed decision to keep the lad in one place? 'Traveling and exploration are important parts of education', Ebube cooed like a sacrificial lamb pleading for mercy before the Gods. He knew quite certainly that someone and something of immense importance was being sacrificed on the altar of fears, to the Gods of fear. It was obi and his promising future, his development spheres, exposure and explorations were being truncated. Frankly speaking, between the prohibition or embargo from the use of phone and the deliberate restriction and attachment to just one place, it was dire difficult to tell which of the two vexed Ebube more. Yet, it was not just the vexation that mattered most for Ebube.

There was more to just how he felt or his emotions. The anger was minimal and manageable. At most, in the space of days or weeks, the pain and anger he felt terribly in his heart would give way to normal life. But the consequence and negative implication and long-term damage that would result from such a decision/judgment in the life of Obi (affecting negatively his diverse development, maturity, sophistications) would be so hard, if not impossible, to undo, resolve and redeem. Restraining and putting Obi in one place, because he should be disciplined, would deny and rob him of many things in life. It was not for the uncle the best of decision and judgment. He saw it as an understated and refined way of enthroning the maxim of 'borrowing from Peter in order to pay Paul,' or even worse still, 'penny wise yet pound foolish'. Ebube could not just find it easy to have his head think through how a child at this present Age and time would have to pass all his formative years and studies in one single place without moving out and experiencing other environments chiefly because of fear of losing the child to any sorts of wrong lifestyle – real or imagined – but most times, imaginary. Ironically, they did not fear the level of damage and danger that resulted from such a parochial and circumscribed culture which cripples and paralyses and thwarted learning and advancements due to very limited interactions with other parts of the world.

Ebube was certain too that apart from Obi's case, many people did this and even took satisfaction in doing so. But he saw it as a serious way to damage a person, to gain or achieve so little from life without helping the victims to build a diverse relationship, diverse encounters, diverse knowledge, diverse world to broaden the horizon of life, the horizon of progress and to develop and possess a larger picture and perspective about reality. Such victims were quite easy to be spotted out particularly in eventuality of handling situations, encountering new cultures, changes and adaptation. They might not even survive it. At best, they do very little or poorly.

In the end, virtually everyone saw reason with Ebube. His opinions were largely considered. Despite this huge progress gained from the lingered family congress, the same eldest member of the family kept calling, fruitlessly, for the dance of the lion as ultimate decider of whether Obi should live or die; whether he should be cleansed and deleted from the holy fold being devoured and eaten up by the fierce lion or be spared. For one thing, the old man was very troubled and pained that the old tradition of the family was being flouted, swept away, undermined, ignored and abandoned. For what it was, he hated passionately to think that bearing his indigenous culture has been described and ascribed and proscribed as from the pit of hell. And all that made sense and was celebrated as authentic and valid, and what satisfied the way to life and God was removing his garments and clinging to white man's own. He fought fruitlessly the belief that being western or possessing western character was the only certified and valid assessment and expression of reality, the parameter and measuring stick for good life including finding God. And ancestral picture or identity was understood and treated as from the pit of hell which everyone had to and readily stayed away from and avoided like the evil forest; they disassociated and disentangled themselves from it; they renounced and denounced it with pentecostal energy, fervency and excitement.

It became a thing of glamour and splendour to be westernized in names and others. And conversely, it was extremely repugnant, impiety, satanic, taboo, outlaw and disdainful to be known otherwise, to still identify with the ancestral life instrumentalized in the dance of the lion. It was a thing of pride and glory and social status and piety to be western in identity. And it was a curse and evil foundation and evil fate to be ancestral. One day, the entire community was challenged by a wise man or rather a drunkard who told them how ancestral the other was to the owners. Some were too quick, after listening to the beggar-drunk, to take to cheap excitement and judgment thinking that the spectacular event of that day would initiate and engender a positive change in the tradition of hostility to ancestral life and general traditions and cultures of the people. But it never did.

The old man, from all indications particularly his weight of experiences, was to bear extremely the symbol of wisdom, the custodian of the traditions of the people.Yet, a lot of people did not see this wisdom or any acclaimed vision of old age perspicacity traditionally symbolized in bearing white hair. On the contrary, if anything at all was seen in him, it was rather an acute fear, subtle phobia that had lingered for long and held him spell-bound and hexed for decades of years and held the community captives for centuries of years in the old tradition of the dance of the lion. It was the ultimate fear of not knowing how to come out of the old habit and to embrace the new. The same ultimate fear that has kept many for years in their old habits and disdainful way of life. The fear was even heightened the more by the same man who kept reminding the entire house of the awaited disaster and other dire consequence if they departed from the old tradition of the dance of the lion. The old man wanted to still see the past in the present. He wanted history to repeat itself. But history is a continuation not definitely a repetition. A continuation in different modes. It was Pat that did his utmost best to prove to him that the old tradition of the dance of the lion has continued in a different form. Pat did not fail to continue to maintain his stance that Christ is the ultimate lion, the lion of the tribe of Judea.

But for Ebube, it was different. Or he added (more wisdom) to what Mr Pat has said. Ebube told the elderly man that day that the new lion which will cleanse Obi, the family and the entire universe is the digital sphere which all and sundry must come close to, not to fear, not to run and chide away from but to dance around it and celebrate it. Because no one can truly fly without modern technology, without phone gadgets in our own time and space. The only remaining option is to stay and wallow in caves and captivity, suffer bondage and backwardness. He cooed and pleaded, 'say NO to reckless adventures. Say YES to progressive and liberating adventures'.

163

POSTSCRIPT

Ebube had also long seen and complained, outside his own family,concerning such ugly and disturbing culture of delayed and denied education and diverse development at that, which have endured among many people who did not do well to expose their kids and wards to early learning because of age and fear of safety and they ended up only wasting or making such people to lag extensively behind. Though, they learnt things in life but so belatedly and they never did as much as they would have accomplished *parisparsi*. They failed to develop their capacities fully and satisfactorily.

For the few weeks he had been at home, he was disturbed by the story of a family that insisted that the daughter would only go to learn a skill after her secondary school. Ebube wanted young people to learn so much from their tender age, to be given generously to exposure with open mind and not certainly the usual refined phobia, shallow and narrow-mindedness that cripple and paralyses and obstruct learning and growth adversely. He appraised still the condition of the neighbour notwithstanding its glaring porosity, deficiency and weakness; compared to other worse situation where most people only wake up to it after graduating from the university or even after marriage and having gone so far in life. For such people, the learnings and skills they acquired were, not essentially part of who they were or their life, but only for damage control, to make up for what they should and could have done while much younger.

To Ebube, it was not the best of the decision.'Why wait until after college when the various holidays particularly long summer holidays could be used in advancing and achieving different courses in skill acquisitions and capacity building?'Ebube inquired rhetorically. That was what Ebube thought was the best thing to do in a modern and sophisticated society. It would enable the person to have enough capacities, learning, marketable skills and exposure and not until when into the university or afterwards as the case maybe. He was even much more disturbed learning that certain higher institutions, religions and cultures for the reason of morality or obedience still adapted the old culture of not permitting their adult students to use computers, phones and access internet. They do not integrate it into the training and upbringing of young ones to grant them the freedom to go out, explore, have experiences and learn and grow better. Rather, they preferred cloistral and reclusive existence of shallow experience, timid exposure and limited world.

All this stayed and settled in his thought early in the morning before he finally rose, stretched and joined the family for morning assembly and prayer. It was his last day in the house. He was travelling the next day to Russia to formally engage Sophia's family and begin the marriage processes. He returned with her after a month for permanent settlement in Nigeria. Works were already made available for the two intelligent couple within their various areas of expertise. They made a very happy home and high-profile accomplishments in their careers.

Ebube's father did not lie when he opted and insisted on his return home to serve and develop the motherland. All the skills, capacities and knowledge beginning with early exposure he had acquired could not be given away cheaply for charity to others despite the traditional phobia of not making it in the homeland. Charity must begin at home. The phobia was conquered.

Obi was a better person with the more open and listening family and life he later experienced and enjoyed. He grew up even a better student who learnt so much from machines and tools. He made his papers in college at first sitting and went into the university. He studied Media and Communication.

ABOUT THE BOOK

Within our own time and space when the power of science has not only circumvented the law of gravity to be able to suspend big and strong metal in the air for hours; but ultimately a time when technological gadgets and microchips are the new toys with which children played with and internet space is the new Greek assembly which virtually everyone attended and participated in, there lived a powerful household called Edoga. DIGITAL SPHERE describes modern technology of phones and gadgets as a school and the attendant phobia with which it is welcomed. Phobia has caused many families like Obi's from endorsing early exposure and explorations and they thought that avoidance, taboos, cutting off, denial and waiting till old age was the working panacea.